BELIEVE IN ME THIS CHRISTMAS MORN

STAR LIGHT ~ STAR BRIGHT SERIES BOOK THREE

L. A. SARTOR

Star Light, Star Bright
The first star I see tonight
I wish I may, I wish I might,
Have the wish I wish tonight.

~ anonymous

This book is for you.
You've believed in this series.
Thank you.

I hope you enjoy Mitch's journey. His story was one I knew I had to write. I couldn't leave him as he was at the end of Be Mine This Christmas Night. He had to find a way to let his guilt go.
(Yes, Let It Go is one of my favorite songs.)

1

"UNCLE MITCH, I WISH YOU WERE COMING TOO," PETER Evans whispered.

Mitchell Thomas hid his smile, quite sure that his nephew had no idea just how awkward an uncle coming along on a honeymoon would be.

Glancing toward the newly created family waiting for Peter on the curb under the awning at Denver International Airport, Mitch acknowledged the pain that was always present, but more so today. Cole, his brother-in-law, wrapped his arm around his wife of a few hours, Annie Hamilton-Evans, and Annie wrapped her arm around Josh, Cole's younger son and Mitch's other nephew.

Mitch took a breath and pushed away the feeling of now being a fifth wheel in the family. "How about you bring me home a shell, the prettiest one you can find," he said, not wanting to make Peter feel bad about going to Hawaii.

"Deal," the boy said.

Mitch wrapped him in a quick goodbye hug, then watched as his nephew ran to the curb, and Annie came to the SUV to get the last bag, a huge carry-on filled with what, he couldn't imagine. Probably stuff to keep the boys occupied on the long flight to Hawaii.

Mitch handed her the bag.

"Thanks for bringing us to the airport," Annie said, hefting the carry-on to her shoulder. "I know today was hard for you, and I was pretty sure you wanted to be anywhere but around us for another hour or so, yet you offered to bring us to the airport."

"I had to be here anyway, so it all worked out."

Mitch braved Annie's searching look, knowing she was thinking *yeah, right. Stop fooling around with me.* She was a hard woman to fool. "You're getting covered in the white stuff." He forced a smile, trying to keep the conversation light.

"Doesn't matter. Did you know that even before the wedding, the boys wondered if you'd be okay today? Josh was pretty darn worried about you. And Peter wanted you to walk me down the aisle instead of him."

His two nephews meant everything to him, and to know they were thinking about him at all today made his cheek muscles relax into a genuine smile.

"I'm fine. Really. Enjoy the islands. It will be a different kind of honeymoon, but I'm glad you're making the boys a part of it."

"You know Cole and I wouldn't have it any other way.

Last night Pete asked about how 'my first mom' might be feeling about this. And I've got to admit, for once I didn't have an answer that sounded right."

Mitch pushed away the pang of sorrow that still snagged his heart even though Lauren had been dead three years. The reality was that his sister was gone and his nephews couldn't do any better than have Annie as their stepmom. "First and foremost, Lauren would have wanted the boys to be happy and secure. That's what I told him when he asked me."

This time his smile wasn't forced as Annie's eyebrows shot toward her hairline.

From the corner of his eye Mitch saw Cole, still on the curb, waving his finger in a circle, indicating it was time to wrap this up and get Annie moving.

"Go, Cole looks like he needs you. Have a safe flight."

"You, too. By the way, I think the website contest was a cool idea, the winner is really lucky to get you."

Annie stood on her tippy toes, and Mitch bent to receive her kiss on the cheek. Then he watched as she hurried to her new family. The foursome turned around to wave goodbye, then headed inside the terminal.

Another zing to his heart. He heard himself sigh and hated how lonely he felt at this moment.

Mitch got back into his new Lexus and headed toward the airport's parking lot. He wasn't going to be gone more than a couple of days max, working on the website of his contest winner. So he picked the close-in parking, figuring the cost wouldn't be outrageous for that short time. And with amazing luck, he got a space on his first time around the maze of the multistoried parking structure.

After entering DIA's terminal, a two-hour delay greeted him at the departure board, lengthened from the hour he'd seen when he checked the flight status on his phone before leaving Boulder.

Mitch didn't want another drink after all the glasses of champagne at the wedding reception, but he didn't want coffee either. So he headed for the ice cream shop in the main terminal, thinking about his nephews and their love of ice cream, on any day, in any weather.

They took after Lauren. But while they and Lauren loved anything with the word chocolate in it, he was partial to anything with nuts and caramel.

Sitting in front of his double-scoop bowl of caramel nut cluster with, in honor of the boys, a healthy dose of hot fudge on top, he dug in. Savoring the mix of flavors, he tried to focus on the website needs of his contest winner before their up-coming meeting.

Belle Grantham currently lived in Pagosa Springs, Colorado, and had won his contest. The prize was that he'd create a website for the winner and maintain it for a year. Her nonprofit literacy project, Goal 100% ~ Literacy for Women, was in desperate need of a boost.

Yep, she needed him. Mitch's website company was tops in the industry. He could pick and choose his clients, something that still blew his mind. Eleven years ago, he'd barely made ends meet in expensive Denver when he'd left Web Wizards and decided to go solo, creating his own company, It's Alive Web Design.

Mitch glanced at his phone clock and realized he'd been sitting for over an hour in front of a whistle-clean ice cream bowl. He'd better head for the gate. This season, a week before Christmas, security wasn't speedy even in the TSA pre-qualified line. By the time he got to the gate, they were calling his row to board. Onward to Durango, Colorado, to pick up his rental car, drive the sixty miles to Pagosa Springs, and meet Belle Grantham.

THE AIRPORT IN DURANGO WASN'T LARGE, AND THERE WERE only a few flights to this Western-slope Colorado town throughout the day. Nevertheless, Belle's palms were moist with fear that she'd miss connecting with Mitchell Thomas before he left the terminal to drive to Pagosa Springs.

The paper sign she'd carefully printed in bold letters with his name was wilting where she clutched it. She shouldn't be the least bit worried—after all, this could be an important detour, and she was sure Mitchell would understand once she told him. Belle knew what she was proposing wasn't like asking him to fly to the moon, but neither did she want to alienate him. She knew Goal 100% desperately needed a new website.

Which would translate to *a lot* more donations. Belle couldn't, wouldn't, allow her baby to go belly up. But the harsh reality was that she couldn't afford to continue much longer as things stood at the moment.

So when one of her board members, Armstrong

Worth, or Armie to a select few, said he needed to meet with her about a large donation, she jumped at the chance. As he was her oldest friend, she was delighted to meet with him.

She just didn't want to do this right now and have her attention divided. She'd wanted to focus singularly on Mitchell Thomas's website ideas.

Belle let loose a soft, tired sigh, realizing just how bone-weary she really was. Goal 100% was a one-woman operation. Sure she had volunteers running the centers and doing the tutoring, but it was all on her to do everything else. Fund-raising, office work, flying out to train the tutors, print the materials. The list really was endless.

Yet it was the passion of her life. She needed more money to bring in some help, even part time. Thus the importance of keeping Mitchell Thomas happy.

As the first of the passengers exited the security area, Belle bucked up, pasted on a bright smile, and held the sign high.

"I'm Mitchell Thomas," a deep voice said from her right.

She turned to look at the tall man in front of her, and her mouth suddenly felt full of hot, dry rocks.

She'd expected a nerd. The man in front of her wasn't anything like the picture on his own website. While she was all of five-feet-nine inches, Mitchell stood at least three inches taller. And damn if he wasn't tripping her switches with the slight cleft in his five o'clock-shaded chin.

In his photograph, he'd worn black-rimmed glasses. Now, sans the frames, his electric blue eyes studied her with an intensity that slightly unnerved her. An unusual position for her to be in.

Basically, she realized, he didn't look the type of person to be led around and cajoled as she was going to have to do to get him back on a plane.

She'd miscalculated big time. "Belle Grantham—"

"Yes, I know."

She blinked, taken aback again. Belle hastily released one side of the paper to wipe her damp palm on her jeans, then stuck her hand out in greeting.

Mitchell grasped it in a firm, single shake and released it. He tilted his head just a tad as if to study her.

"I saw your picture on your website, which by the way, doesn't do you justice. But we'll fix that. What I don't know is what you're doing here. Aren't I supposed to be meeting with you in Pagosa Springs for the next couple of days? Did you decide to be my chauffeur?"

Belle swallowed hard. What she was about to tell Mitchell had all sounded so simple when Armie had proposed his plan to her over the phone a few hours ago.

Now it sounded impossible.

"I needed to catch you before you left the airport." Belle forced herself to maintain eye contact with him for the bombshell she was going to drop. "I have to catch the last flight to Denver." She glanced at the clock on the wall above her. "Which leaves in about twenty minutes. They've already started the boarding call."

Belle bit her lower lip as she watched his brows arch in

surprise, then furrow in worry above those damn fine eyes in the span of a few seconds. The first emotion she could understand, but why the look of worry? Unless he hated to fly.

Uh-oh.

Or maybe it was anger that made his brows come together over his nose.

Double uh-oh. Not a good way to start this crucial business relationship.

"You want me to fly back to Denver?"

"I already have our tickets. We just need to go through security again. I can explain it on the way," she said, rushing her words, feeling less and less in control.

"How about explaining the pertinent points now? The flight over was horrible with the weather. Is this a family crisis?"

He raised a brow, waiting for her answer, and Belle knew instinctively nothing but the truth would do. "No, thankfully it's not family per se. Have you heard of Armstrong Worth?" She expected a nod and received it. Nearly anyone who watched any news feed or broadcast knew of Armie.

To Belle he was simply the guy she went to elementary school with back in the Hill Country of Texas. Then on to private secondary school, each telling their parents they'd quit school if they couldn't go to the same one.

He was the boy—almost man—of eighteen, who escorted her to her debutante ball and the one who splashed her unmercifully in the pool at her papa's Trickle Creek ranch, or his dad's Circle W Doubled ranch.

"Well, Armie is a close friend and he's on the board of my nonprofit." Belle continued her explanation to Mitchell and watched his nod. Of course he'd known—it would make sense that he'd done research on her and the nonprofit.

"He specifically changed his travel plans to a huge economic summit in London to make a short layover at DIA, of course not checking with me first. But he did this so he could meet with me about Goal 100% once he learned..." She trailed off and shied away from looking directly at Mitchell's piercing blue eyes.

"Go on, I don't bite," he said, then smiled as if to make his point.

Mitchell was wrong about the biting. He had the whitest, strongest teeth she'd ever see. And at the country club near Austin, near where she grew up and where everyone whitened and straightened, that was saying something.

"Once he learned that Goal 100% was nearly broke."

MITCH RUBBED HIS CHIN, FEELING THE ROUGHNESS OF HIS five o'clock shadow. He bit down on his frustration at having his carefully wrought plans thrown to the wind all because of a rich guy who crooked his little finger. The last thing he wanted to do was head back to Denver and then Boulder and the memories he was escaping. "You've got a powerful guy on your side. But why does he need to meet with you? Why can't he just have this discussion via phone?"

Just then the intercom blasted the last boarding call for the flight to Denver. Mitch glanced at Belle.

A touch of panic flared in her eyes. "Mitchell, I know this is a huge inconvenience. But this meeting may be as important to me as winning your contest. Together, a new website and what I'm hoping could be an infusion of cash could really make the nonprofit viable until it gets legs and becomes huge. And I figured we could work in your neck of the woods as easily as mine."

Yeah, but I don't want to be in my neck of the woods, Ms. Belle Grantham.

Mitch, fighting his frustration, looked over Belle's head as the last of his fellow passengers exited out of the security area into the terminal. He didn't relish getting back on an airplane, but if she really needed to see this guy and wasn't going to be around to help him, the point of his being here was moot.

"Let's go."

Belle smiled with relief, and unexpectedly his irritation over the high-handedness of Armstrong Worth's tactics fled. Her eyes turned from hazel to almost emerald in color. Dimples appeared in her cheeks, and she was simply gorgeous.

Mitch looked at her more closely.

She wore a black cashmere sweater, jeans that looked distressed but he bet cost a fortune, black knee-high boots, and a pale lavender ski parka that boasted a fancy name.

Her clothes alone were the cost of a first class airplane ticket to...Hawaii.

Her deep auburn hair, cut in a sleek bob that ended just below her chin, swung like rippling satin as she bent down and hoisted a huge leather satchel over one shoulder.

He hadn't noticed the bag sitting on the floor next to her or he'd have offered to carry it for her. *What was it with women and their huge satchels?* A slight grin curved his lips upward.

Belle cocked her head, questioning the reason for his smile, and he refused the invitation to tell her. She led the way to security. They were the only two people in line, so it took but a minute to go through the checkpoint.

The gate was close enough to fast-walk—even so, they were the last passengers to board the small jet. Luckily the flight was only partially filled, so they had their choice of seats. Belle led the way to the back and took the last row, away from the other handful of passengers.

They belted in, taxied, and in minutes were climbing through the clouds and the unrelenting snow. The jet shuddered a bit, did a belly-dropping bump, and then leveled out.

Belle clutched the armrests so tightly her knuckles really were white. He reached across the short space between them and touched her hand. "Are you going to be okay?"

"I'm not the best flier. Or at least not on these small jets," she admitted. "If we don't have any more of those sickening drops, I'll be fine. Thanks for asking."

Mitch pitied her wan smile. He didn't like this kind of flying either, but thought of it as inconvenient rather than defying death.

"Oh,"—Belle interrupted his thoughts—"I forgot to mention that Armie said he'll reimburse you for your flight over to Durango, and of course he paid for these tickets."

Nope. No way in hell was Mitch going to take a dime from "Armie" Worth. "Thanks, but I don't need him to reimburse me for anything." He watched in slight amusement as Belle's brow furrowed and her mouth opened, then shut. He wasn't going to argue this point. Additionally, he'd figure out a way for "Armie" to get his money back for this flight's ticket as well. After all, a guy had his pride.

"However," Mitch continued. "I am surprised that Goal 100% is nearly broke. Your spreadsheet listed only a few expenses, and it didn't look financially unsound. You have a regular, dependable donation coming in each month, although I'm not sure how that person got through the donation process on your website. I tried, but I couldn't get through the screens and gave up.

"Cleaning up your website should help in a big way. It *is* pretty awful. It's bland, doesn't inspire confidence, and lacks a singular focus."

The minute those words left his mouth, he cringed inwardly, wanting to stuff them back in his mouth. God, he was a pain in the ass at times.

"Wow, is that all that's wrong with it?"

But instead of the woman sitting next to him

appearing to be thunderously mad over his foot-in-mouth statement, she laughed. A clear, lovely sound. Not haughty or imperious, which was what he'd expected after learning more about her once she'd won the contest.

For Belle Grantham was pretty simple to sum up. She was a Texas Hill Country, mega-ranch, rich girl. She was Country Club, had made her debut in the traditional formal way, and gone to Wellesley.

She was everything he wasn't.

Yet her concept of the nonprofit Goal 100%~Literacy for Women touched a chord inside him. The cause was something both he and Lauren vehemently believed in.

"That's why I was so pleased to win your contest. As I thought Armie, Papa, and my brother would be. Papa and Junior make up the rest of the board of Goal 100%."

He knew that but figured he'd said enough for the time being.

Belle picked at the leather on the armrest, looked out the window, and finally at him. "The fund looks like it's in the black because I've been the one making that regular donation from my trust fund. This way, all the other donations go to the literacy centers that are up and running. I add the extra money that's needed to fill the gaps."

Mitch couldn't believe what he was hearing. Belle was using her own money to keep the nonprofit afloat?

"I live pretty simply in the Pagosa Springs ranch house the family uses for summer vacations, and the rent on the office space, as you know since you studied my spreadsheet, is nominal. Nevertheless, the real donations are small, pitifully small."

That he could help with. But he was still stuck on the fact that she funded her own nonprofit and did the work of an entire staff. He felt a tiny bit of the stereotype of a rich county-club girl he held against her evaporate.

He focused back on Belle's words.

"But they, as the board, have apparently realized that I'm funding the nonprofit and that it's a pretty shaky endeavor. I get that. I never intended to always use my trust fund. Frankly I thought the donations would be handling all the expenses now. The board has been making subtle hints about changing things, which is why I'm so grateful you chose me as your winner. I just need more time."

Her green eyes took on a militant look, and Mitch chuckled inwardly, figuring Belle wasn't someone to cross.

The jet did another stomach-flopping drop. "God, I hate flying in these planes. I'm going to make Armie bump up his donation just for that reason alone."

Laughter burst from Mitch's lips. After they got done meeting with Worth, Mitch knew the next few days working with Belle would be more interesting than the hours spent with most of his clients.

Which reminded him that he needed to call and cancel his reservations at the hotel right next to Pagosa Springs's famous hot springs. He'd been interested in trying the various thermal pools at differing temperatures but figured it could hold for another time.

A second later he realized that Belle would need a place to stay for the duration of their work, and it obviously couldn't be with him. It would be totally inappropriate for him to host a client.

And the fact that she's a stunning woman has nothing to do with it, right?

Of course. It's simply a matter of no room at the Inn.

Liar.

2

As their flight landed she realized it wasn't simply convincing Mitchell to accompany her that set Belle's nerves up a few notches. She wasn't at all sure this meeting would go in her favor.

They left the jetway and she rolled her shoulders feeling her belly tighten just a bit, her usual physical manifestation of gearing up to do battle.

"Excuse me, can you point the way to the United Lounge," Belle asked a porter pushing an empty wheelchair in the incredibly busy United Airlines concourse at Denver International Airport.

"Yes, ma'am. Just keep going down until you're near Gate 32. It's not far."

"Thanks." Belle gave him a smile, shouldered her satchel, and linked her arm through Mitchell's so not to lose him in the crush of holiday and skiing travelers at the airport.

"Want me to carry that?"

"No, but thanks. I'm used to it."

Then he surprised her by taking the lead, pressing through the crowds with an apologetic smile to those he maneuvered around, taking the sting out of his actions. She almost felt protected. A nice feeling as it seemed she always took control with her circle of friends.

Except for Armie.

She hadn't seen her best friend for over a year, and that was a long time for them not to be face to face. There was no romance, just the comfort of old friends. Akin to wearing super-soft old flannel jammies.

Comfortable.

Then why do you feel you have to gear up for this meeting?

Because maybe she had it all wrong. Her board's rumbles about make it or quit might be more serious than she anticipated. Maybe he wasn't going to help her with a donation that would keep her afloat until she could restructure her fund-raising.

Maybe Armie was going to try and convince her, one way or another, that she had to stop using her own money to fund the nonprofit.

She had to convince *him* that she was taking the steps to make it viable.

The website was obviously a great first step. But she knew she needed some star power behind her fund.

Wait. Maybe Armie was telling her he was going to lend his name to the cause instead of being so behind-the-scenes.

Too many maybes.

She and Mitchell found the club door and she released

his arm. "That was nice. Thanks for buffering through the crowd."

"My pleasure. Are you ready?"

Belle looked at him with surprise. "Why wouldn't I be? Armie's my best friend, not a dream killer." She injected as much confidence as she could into her voice.

Mitchell smiled with raised brows, indicating, she assumed, that he didn't quite believe her.

"Because we're talking about your *dream*, not just friends chatting over drinks. And obviously what he needed to talk to you about couldn't be said over the phone." Then Mitch opened the door for her.

This man had manners reminiscent of the men of Texas.

But polite or not, his words churned up her anxiety again. She pasted on the smile she reserved just for Armie and hid her jitters behind it.

"Hi," Belle greeted the man in the United Airlines uniform at the desk in the front of the club. "Armstrong Worth is expecting us."

"He's in our meeting room. Let me show you the way."

She felt Mitch's hand rest lightly on the small of her back as she followed the attendant. It seemed a bit possessive, and oddly, after a second's thought, she didn't mind.

The attendant opened the door and ushered them in with a sweep of his hand, then quietly closed the door behind them.

Armie sat at a gleaming, oval, oak conference table, working two phones. Within easy reach, a squat glass of ice held two fingers of golden liquid. He looked up and a huge smile spread across his devilishly handsome face.

Often people mistook him for Jon Bon Jovi, and he'd usually laugh in protest while signing their whatevers—including, he said, the T-shirt of a well-endowed woman—with his own name. Then he'd hear the recognition squeal once again. Armstrong Worth was a celebrity in his own right.

Belle had been with him a couple of times it had happened, and she was amazed at his patience.

Her best buddy put down both cell phones and stood. Belle dropped her satchel and ran into his open arms. It felt like coming home. How could she have thought Armie would do anything to harm her?

"Before we get down to brass tacks, let me introduce you to Mitchell Thomas," she said in a rush.

Mitchell moved forward, hand extended. The men were the same height. Their handshake was firm. Belle quickly glanced at their faces and didn't see any tension. Just curiosity. They sized each other up and apparently didn't dislike what they saw.

"Good to meet you, Mitch. You've built quite a reputation in the web design world," Armie said. "Thank you for being so flexible and accommodating my schedule. I know you're a busy man. Meeting with Belladonna, er, Belle, was important, and this was my only chance until the end of the year. And it sounded like the end of the year might be too late."

Belle stood stock still. That didn't sound good at all.

She vaguely heard the knock on the door and the

attendant entering with a tray in his hands and waited until he left to continue this...conversation.

"Not too late. I think I can convince papa and a few of my *friends*," she stressed, "to dig a little deeper into their pockets until the nonprofit gets legs. Gotta tell you, these past few years of financial hardship make fund-raising even more difficult."

He has to understand, I want to make this work. It's important for me, for Mama, and for the idea. No Grantham ever throws in the towel. Ever.

She wasn't stupid about money, and using her trust fund's semiannual distributions was seed money to get the fund going. Belle needed Mitch's website and Armie's influence.

Goal 100% had already funded literacy programs in rural communities in Texas, New Mexico, and Oklahoma with rousing success. Three states out of fifty, 32 million people who had low literacy skills in the United States alone. It was daunting. But a Grantham never shied away from any challenge.

"I think you're pretty close to being too late," Armie said. "And yes, we know that it was your monthly donations keeping the fund afloat. We also know just how worn out you are, running this on a thread, being the chief cook and bottle washer.

"Dutch called me last night and wanted to run the idea past me about you closing your fund and finding an already established fund that you can lend your name to."

"Papa has not said any of that to me." She pointed at her chest with a finger that was trembling so badly, she quickly put her hands in her pocket. This was far worse than she could ever have anticipated.

"He wouldn't, right?" Armie said softly. "Your dad wouldn't want to hurt his baby girl, and he knows I don't mind being the bearer of the board's news."

Belle shook her head; this wasn't right. "You've voted on this? Without me present?"

"No, not yet. That's where the end of the year comes in."

"Papa would tell me to my face, Armie. He's never shied away from letting me know if I was doing something wrong, but then, yes, he'd tell me how to fix it. So, whose idea was this really—"

Armie held up his hand, then checked his Rolex. "I've got about ten minutes, so I want to outline my plan quickly, and if we have time, we can toss around the specifics."

MITCH HATED WITH A PASSION THE GESTURE OF HOLDING UP a hand to shut someone off. His parents used it all the time when he needed to talk to them. That, of course, was only when they were home. Which was rarely to practically never.

So he wasn't surprised that at Armie's interruption, her eyes narrowed and the green gaze turned glittery hard.

It was more than anger Belle was holding in. Mitch saw the pain in her eyes. This wasn't at all what she'd hoped this meeting would be about. It didn't sound like a donation was forthcoming.

She crossed her arms over her chest and cocked her head. Obviously she was going to listen, but any more than that was up for grabs.

He felt as if he were at a sparring match. Mitch moved to the étagère, poured a glass of wine, and placed it in front of Belle, thinking she might need it. He then snagged a soda for himself and stood at the end of the oval conference table for a better view.

Worth took a long draw on his whiskey, then put the glass down with a thunk. "I have a million-dollar check written out to Goal 100%, ready for you to deposit—"

"But?"

"You know me so well. Here's the deal. If you're not going to close the fund, then what I and your dad think would be best for you and the fund is for you to hire some professional staff. That means moving your headquarters away from Pagosa Springs and into say, Denver, Dallas, or even Austin. You're not going to get the talent you need by asking them to relocate to such a small town."

"You know I can't afford to hire 'talent' and certainly not the rent for the type of up-to-date space anyone of the caliber you suggest would demand."

Mitch noticed the soft Texas twang in Belle's voice grew more pronounced the more agitated she became. And the more precise Worth became as he outlined his plan.

"I have office space in both Denver and Austin. I'll lease it to you for a dollar a year for the first five years. The million will go a long way to paying expenses and funding your project. However, the professionals I've already talked to will require specific changes to make the nonprofit function to its max."

"And it'll no longer be truly mine."

Belle's voice dropped to just above a whisper and told Mitch everything he needed to know about Belle and her project. This was more than a simple nonprofit: Goal 100% had deep significance to her, and she wanted to run it to keep that importance intact.

Again he felt that pang of guilt over his assumption that she was merely a rich girl with a hobby.

"Of course it will be. Don't be stubborn, Belladonna," Worth said with, Mitch noted, a trace of impatience. "This is a great opportunity to move the nonprofit into high gear. And you'll have a new website courtesy of Mitch to add another layer of legitimacy."

"And what's in it for you and your million dollars, Armie? Are you looking for a cause to become philanthropic about? Following the steps of the likes of Bill Gates and Warren Buffet?"

"Not that rich, as you know, but yes. Why not your fund versus somebody else's?"

"So your cool million comes with silk strings attached."

"I'd hoped we'd have an agreement before I had to leave, but my offer stands until the end of the year." He got up and knocked back the remainder of his whiskey. "Finish up the wine, please eat the food. I have the meeting room for a while yet. And Mitch, after you're done with Belle's site, I'd like to talk to you about a couple of mine. I think they could be better."

"Sure, I'd be happy to take a look at them," Mitch said, wondering if the man was merely throwing him a carrot.

Worth bent to kiss Belle's cheek.

She stiffened. The opposite of the hug she'd thrown herself into only thirty minutes ago.

"I'll call you from London in a couple of days. I know this is a short time frame, but it's better to pull off the band aid quickly, right? If you have questions, call me and leave a message."

Mitch put down his soda and wiped his hands on a napkin just as Worth turned to him and stuck out his hand.

His handshake was firm and his smile genuine; then he was gone and the room became very quiet.

Mitch glanced at Belle. She picked up her glass and sipped the wine, her grip on the stem so tight he thought it might snap. "The new website design will help, but finding the kind of sponsorship Worth is offering you is pretty hard to turn down."

His ploy worked. The unhappiness in her gaze fled as a mutinous gleam replaced it. She sat straighter in her chair, back ramrod stiff.

"Not for me, it isn't. I know Armie, and though he says it'll still be mine, it won't, and I'm not ready to give up this dream. It was Mama's dream as well, and Papa knows that. So let's get to work. The sooner my website is up, the faster you can get to Armie's job."

The cynicism in her voice took him aback. "Belle, your job is my priority right now. Not Worth's, not anyone's but yours. We can't get back to Pagosa Springs tonight, and really, now that we're on this side of the divide, let's stay on this side and get it done. Finding you a hotel room shouldn't be too hard."

IT WAS THE WEEK BEFORE CHRISTMAS. THERE MIGHT BE A hotel room available in Boulder after a dozen or so calls, but Belle wasn't going to go through that kind of nonsense if she didn't have to.

She pulled her cell phone out of her satchel, dialed, then put the phone on speaker. One thing she hated with this indispensable modern piece of technology was the way people held private conversations in front of their friends or companions without regard to how rude it was. It drove her crazy. She wasn't going to do that to Mitchell.

The phone on the other end rang and rang. Damn, she didn't think about Maisie not picking up. Thankfully, her buddy from the second ranch over and across the river from theirs finally answered.

Belle swallowed her anger over Armie's high-handedness and put a cheerful tone into her voice. "Maisie, hi, it's Belle. I'm in Colorado. I need a favor. Do your folks still own that cabin at Chautauqua Park in Boulder?"

"Belle," Maisie squealed. "I've missed your emails—you must be super busy with your nonprofit. Sure they still have the cabin. Why?"

Belle glanced at Mitch, wondering what he was thinking about her just taking over the hunt for her accommodations. Then she didn't care. She was on a mission to prove Armie and her father wrong. Every minute needed to be focused on making this step work.

Mitch seemed interested in their conversation but unconcerned as he made a cracker sandwich of cheese and prosciutto.

"Can I rent it for a couple of days?"

"Belle, don't be silly. It's yours for as long as you need it. We have a Realtor lock box on the back door. The combo is 226. Although," Maisie laughed, "I saw on the weather channel that it's nearly a blizzard there, and the back door is down a slope and up the stairs to a porch."

"I remember. You're a gem, really."

"How's the nonprofit going?"

"Great," Belle said, forcing energy into her voice. "I'm working with a new web designer to update the site. Check it out after Christmas. I'll send you the link again."

"I will. Oh, and in the cabin, you'll need to crank up the heat on the furnace and water heater, and turn on the fridge. There's no food or coffee, and I know you're a coffee junkie. But markets are close by. Enjoy it and next time you're in the Bay area, please say you'll do lunch."

"You're on. I've missed you." And Belle realized she really did. The words weren't simply the usual platitudes. "I want to come and see a ballet at the War Memorial Opera House and your new real estate office, so you're on for more than lunch. Maybe a house-guest for a day or two."

"Deal."

"Merry Christmas, Belle, Maisie," they said

simultaneously. Belle smiled again as she disconnected the call.

"Okay, one problem solved." She licked her finger and made a check mark in the air. Talking to Maisie somehow brought her out of her defeat, and she bucked up, knowing she wasn't going down without a fight.

The light of battle filled her, and she harnessed it, knowing that when she was alone, she'd hurt, as her trust in Armie, her papa, and her brother was mightily bruised.

"How do we get to Boulder? Taxi? Shuttle?" she asked Mitchell.

The satisfaction Belle felt at his confused look in the turnabout of her mood made her even stronger. "Mitchell, I'm going to fight this—they can't take Goal 100% away from me."

"Okay then, I'm in your corner."

Wow, that filled her with warmth and even more energy to win this. "Is one of those mine?"

"You're hungry?"

"A warrior needs food. And yes, actually I am. I haven't eaten since midmorning."

She took the other cracker sandwich Mitch held out to her and ate it in two bites.

"In answer to your question, we're getting to Boulder in my SUV. I parked it close to the terminal, thinking I wouldn't be gone long. Little did I know."

He chuckled and Belle felt it tingle all the way down to her toes.

"Want another one?" He gestured to the stack of cracker sammies he'd created.

"Am I that obvious?"

"Only by the drool on the corner of your chin."

She laughed and damn if it didn't feel good. Mitch's brand of humor was exactly what she needed at this moment. And if he was doing it so she'd feel better, it was working. She felt better. Even strong. God knows, she needed all the strength she could muster.

Besides, just because she'd always been the person who'd volunteer first, the one who always found a way to make something work, didn't mean she was a patsy. She had pride and she wanted to trust.

Armie just took a large measure of that away.

But right now she began to trust Mitchell Thomas, who was funny, handsome, and bright. Maybe a tad outspoken, but she was used to that from her papa and brother.

"I take it from your conversation with Maisie that you've been to Boulder?" Mitchell asked as he handed her a napkin and pointed to the corner of his mouth.

Belle dabbed her mouth in the same spot he'd pointed to and washed down the last bite of food with a sip of her wine. "Once my family drove through on our way to Estes Park, then up to Yellowstone. We stopped at this overlook, it was my first view of Boulder. Another time when I spent a couple of weeks with Maisie at their cabin. We hiked in the park and across the mesa all the way over to this research place that looked modern yet ancient sandstone towers—"

"That would be the National Center for Atmospheric Research. Cole, my...brother-in-law has a lab up there."

She noticed the way he hesitated over using brother-in-law status, and his brow furrowed. Why? Family issues? Maybe that's why he was so concerned at the Durango airport when he'd mentioned a family crisis.

"And we hit the mall that's on..." she trailed off, not remembering the name.

"Pearl Street."

Belle snapped her fingers. "Yep, that's it. We floated down the creek in inner tubes and watched the guys on the University of Colorado's football team work out. It was a good"—she drew out the word *go-oo-d*—"summer."

He grinned as she'd hoped.

"Well, now it's all of maybe ten degrees outside," he said. "Snow is falling and piling up on the roads and the mountain trails. The forecasts say this should be going on for another day or so and then again by the next weekend. So it looks like it's going to be a white Christmas."

"That's okay, I love snow. That's one reason I moved to our little ranch house in Pagosa Springs. Want it?" She nodded toward the remaining meat-laden cracker and, after seeing his head-shake, wolfed it down. "Where are you from?"

"East coast. Moved to Denver, then Boulder, a little over eleven years ago."

"You like it then?" She waited for his reply, then was curious about his hesitation in answering.

"Yes, Boulder is an amazing place to live." He poured the last of the wine in her glass and finished his soda.

His voice lacked conviction.

3

Mitch unlocked his SUV and watched Belle put her satchel onto the back seat, then slide into the soft leather front seat.

"This has that indescribable new car smell," Belle said.

"It's only two weeks old. Buckle up."

She didn't move, instead was just looking at the dash with its bold brush of blue lights. He wondered what she was thinking—certainly she'd seen fancier cars than his Lexus Hybrid SUV.

The interior lights dimmed, and he heard the click of her seat belt. They were ready to roll.

"Do you recycle and compost as well?"

Startled, he glanced at her in the darkened car. "Why? Because I drive a hybrid? Yes, I do recycle and I have a composting bin. Did I pass some sort of test?"

"No and yes."

For a split second, his hands tightened on the leather and wood steering wheel. Then he scoffed at himself.

Other people's perceptions shouldn't bother him any longer. He was a self-made man and proud of every accomplishment. Yet he fought to keep the tension out of his voice. "Explain, please."

"No, of course there is no test you need to pass. But Papa is big on recycling and wind energy on the ranch, so doing this will score points with him."

"And do I need to score points with him?" *Ha, what a fool. You thought you didn't care about people's perceptions. You just proved yourself wrong.*

"Of course not, only with me," she said with a light teasing tone.

Which didn't make him feel any better.

"So where is your office?"

He backed out of the parking spot and queued up in the long line to pay for parking as he pondered how to answer her question.

His office? It was his command central, complete with a half dozen monitors, several keyboards, one chair, and one long counter for it all to fit on.

It was a solo haven; he hadn't ever thought of making it a working room for two.

It was also the second of five bedrooms in his big but empty house. That was surely not going to score points with her, as apparently he needed to.

For God's sake man, don't let her pedigree and money change your perspective. You're giving her a website. A great website.

He saluted his internal voice as he paid the attendant

his parking fee. And headed out toward the toll road to Boulder.

"Your office?" Belle repeated.

"Sorry, I did hear you the first time. For the presentations, we'll use my conference room. I can power-point everything up on the screen. I've already created a dummy site to work with so you can see how each page interacts and the information it gives."

"That sounds great, I can't wait to get started. May I ask why you decided on offering this contest? A website makeover for free? I'm sure your staff could have done all of this with you directing them. But to have you, the head honcho do this is...awesome."

He smiled slightly, thanking the universe that Belle, in some ways, gave him an answer he could use convincingly. "You said it. I wanted to do this and I could without its impacting anyone but me."

And the fact that you started planning this the minute you heard the news from Cole and Annie that they were getting married.

Getting away from the wedding was really the idea behind creating the contest, but the boys wanted him there for the ceremony, and really it would have been incredibly insensitive to them and Cole and his new bride not to be there. So he'd planned his getaway to happen right after the reception. He'd opened the contest in May and by December first he'd found his winner.

Belle's nonprofit.

"And your staff doesn't need you this week?"

"I planned this so all the projects were done before the holidays hit."

Vague answer, but at the moment he didn't want to go any deeper into "his staff."

Reality was there was no staff. Mitch knew he was on the cusp of needing a couple of designers, an admin assist to deal with the calls, the bills, and the usual business end stuff Mitch hated. But at the moment, with his hectic schedule, all that was too much to figure out. Let alone look for the right location. And he worried that dealing with the structure of a staff would force him to become a manager and he'd lose the creative control that had made him so successful.

Instead, he worked horrendously long hours and met his clients at the Icarus Office Suites, which offered comfortable, high-tech conference rooms where he could set up his equipment and walk his clients through their sites. In addition Icarus had phone and secretarial support, which was how he dealt with getting out his bills and making appointments.

Which reminded him that it was way too late in the evening to call Icarus for a conference room, so he'd need to call first thing in the morning and hope they had one available for his initial presentation to Belle.

"Well, after Armie's surprise bomb, I need *you* more than ever. Thank you once again."

Mitch glanced at Belle and saw her bite her lower lip just as she turned her head to look out the side window.

Damn if he wouldn't do his best-ever website for her.

There was silence in the car for a long distance. The

wipers effortlessly pushed away the snow that quickly accumulated on the windshield. There were few vehicles on the road, so there was an odd sense of isolation with the snow surrounding them.

Mitch pulled onto US-36, leaving the toll road that made it so easy to get to the airport in Denver. Within minutes he was climbing to the top of Davidson Mesa with Boulder nestled below, but he couldn't see a thing because of the snowfall veiling everything.

"This is the mesa where you stopped years ago to see Boulder for the first time," he said.

"Wow, I can't see anything. That's a shame—I would have liked to see it in the snow."

"Then we'll come up another time. We'll be at your friend's cabin in under ten."

"That's good. What time do you want to meet tomorrow? I can be ready at seven, even earlier if you want."

"It doesn't need to be that early. We still have to find the cabin and get you settled. And I live less than five minutes away from Chautauqua, so it'll be a quick detour to pick you up and off to the office."

She wouldn't need to get up that early, but he'd be up and moving way before seven. And usually by eight, he was on at least his second cup. In fact he loved mornings. Their quiet and sense of new beginning always appealed to him from the time he was old enough to appreciate dawn.

His parents were never up early enough to make him and Lauren breakfast, so he did. Sometimes he got really inspired and made flavored waffles. Lauren had loved to cook, and when she was old enough they would make feasts for their friends...at their friends' houses. He and his sister never brought people to their house. He was too ashamed over its condition. Dirty and dumpy.

"I'll pick you up a little after eight. The offices don't open until then, so there's no need to start earlier."

"Okay, I'll be ready. I'd offer to cook breakfast, but apparently I'll need to go to the market first and get some supplies. So maybe dinner?"

Dinner? Should he eat with her?

Where on earth did your common sense fly to? Of course you can eat dinner with her.

But she's a client.

And? You've had dinner with clients before. Granted they were business deals, but so is this.

Yeah, but none of those clients were as damned attractive as Belle Grantham.

Stop right there. She's beautiful and rich, used to getting anyone and everything she wants. Not your type and never will be.

He turned left from Baseline Road into Chautauqua Park and found Goldenrod Drive and the cabin.

He stared with dismay at the foot plus of snow that covered the walkway up to and around the cabin. Belle's face mirrored his expression.

"Don't worry, I'll get the key from the Realtor box, you stay tight." He pulled on his hat and gloves, and stepped from the warmth of the vehicle. The sharpness of the cold stole his breath. Turning on his phone's flashlight, he fought his way through the snow and down the slight incline to the back of the house, climbed the flight of wooden steps to the realtor's box hanging on the back door. After a bit of coaxing, the combo spun and he grabbed the key.

Using the path he'd just cut through the white stuff, he scrabbled back up to this SUV in half the time and got back into his toasty vehicle. "Damn, it's deep out there. Want me to carry you to the door?"

Where did that come from?

"God, no. You'd break your back and drop me."

"I don't think so. I work out," he said, slightly wounded that she would think him a wimp.

"Thanks, but no. I would appreciate you coming in with me until I make sure I get the heat up. A great website isn't going to do me any good if I'm a Belle Popsicle."

Mitch led the way to the front door, trampling the snow as much as possible to make a path for Belle. Once in the cabin, they immediately got the heat and water heater turned up high and the fridge on.

While waiting for the place to warm up, they checked out the rest of Belle's home-away-from-home with their jackets still on. There were three bedrooms, two bathrooms, and a combined living and dining room space. The rooms were either wood-paneled or plastered and painted a warm honey color to go with the wood. It was charming.

In fact it was far homier than his quadruple-sized house.

They checked out the bigger of the two bedrooms.

Luckily the linens were on the bed and looked ready for Belle to crawl into. He saw her try to stifle a yawn. "The bed looks comfortable, so you'll fall asleep quickly."

She laughed. "I can be asleep under the stars on hard ground with a sleeping bag in five minutes. So this is wonderful."

That surprised the hell out of him. And another preconceived notion bit the dust.

Belle unzipped her pale lavender parka, and he realized it did feel warmer in the cabin.

He went into the kitchen and opened the fridge door, feeling the cool air. Then he turned on the tap, and the water warmed his still-chilled fingers.

"Okay, you're set for the night. Other than coffee, do you have everything you need?"

Belle patted her huge satchel. "I travel light—clothes, makeup, computer, and phone."

"That doesn't look light," he said and lifted the leather bag. "Lord, it's *not* light."

"Maybe for a guy this isn't packing light, but for me, it's really light. Ask my brother—Junior thinks I usually haul gold bricks in my luggage."

"Junior?"

"Yeah. He was supposed to be a girl, so they hadn't even thought of a boy's name. Mama and Papa didn't want to know the sex of their first child, and in her family, girls were always first born. So it was assumed..." She shrugged.

"And how did they come up with Belle?"

"When I was born, Papa called me the belle of the ball, and Mama agreed." Belle laughed. "Can you imagine calling a squalling, red-faced newborn the belle of the ball? I think Papa was happy to finally have a daughter. Mama had two miscarriages between Junior and me, and I think he was just so relieved, he was blind."

Mitch wondered, as he had a million times before, what it would have been like for him and Lauren to have parents who really wanted the children they'd borne.

BELLE COULDN'T GET MITCHELL OUT OF HER MIND AS SHE brushed her teeth, then cleaned her face, and slathered cream over her cheeks.

He was full of surprises. Nice surprises.

He made her laugh, even when she was positive she didn't feel like it.

He'd been courtly on several occasions, including trudging through the snow to get her key to the cabin.

He said he worked out.

She closed her eyes as the fantasy of him sweeping her off her feet, strong arms cradling her against his chest, played in her mind.

And he was handsome, distractingly so.

Knock it off. You're being silly and acting like a teenager.

Well, I haven't dated in over a year. So maybe I should be forgiven.

Okay, you're forgiven, now stop it.

Belle listened to her inner voice and agreed. She was here not only to get a new and powerful website, but to learn how to use it to its maximum advantage and save Goal 100%.

Not to be distracted from her mission.

Suddenly her knees trembled, and she sat on the john's lid before they gave out on her.

How could Armie, Papa, and Junior think of taking Goal 100% away from her?

A black hurt filled her over their lack of confidence. She'd trusted them with her most important endeavor and now worst case, they wanted her to quit. Best case they wanted her to be a figurehead. If that.

They were overreacting about the way she spent her own money. Hell, if she wanted to give to another charity, they wouldn't raise this kind of fuss.

And yes, she was working hard, sometimes spinning her wheels. But there were successes, scores of them.

Where did they get off, trying to push her in a direction she didn't want to go? Why did they do this in such a hurtful way, behind her back?

On shaking legs, she walked the short distance from the bathroom to the bedroom, crawled between the cool sheets and pulled the duvet up to her chin. Shivering, she curled into a fetal position.

Trying to get warm.

Trying to protect her heart.

The people she loved most in the world had broken her trust. Yes, she'd vowed to Mitchell that she would fight, but now, alone in the cabin without his support, all she felt was a heaviness in her soul. She wanted the night to pass quickly and shivered again.

Even the heavy duvet couldn't warm her or take away the shard of ice lodged in her heart.

After leaving Belle at Maisie's cabin in Chautauqua Park, Mitch parked his single car in his three-car garage and entered his house. Immediately something felt off, and he realized that after the vibrancy of being in Belle's presence, his house felt empty and sterile.

His life felt pretty much the same way. The boys were in Hawaii with their new mother, and Mitch had little to look forward to.

Slipping off his boots, he moved surefooted in the dark over the polished oak floors and flipped on the wall switch. In the blinding glare from the recessed ceiling light fixtures, he looked around his abode without his usual blinders, seeing it the way Belle would see it.

He hadn't invested a lot of energy in decorating his digs even though he'd paid top dollar for the house because of its location below Chautauqua Park and its ridiculously huge square footage. He hadn't needed to do much to the house, for he didn't entertain other than his nephews, Peter and Josh.

And for them he had what they needed. A big screen TV, an X-box *and* a PlayStation. And in the freezer, lots of frozen chocolate chip cookie dough, pepperoni pizzas, and chocolate ice cream.

When they visited, one corner of the living room was theirs. Mitch had bought three rocking gamer chairs that could be pulled close to the TV so they could all play video games. And when the boys spent the night, he had a bedroom with two double beds and posters on the walls of their current favorite action heroes.

The rest of the large living room was a mishmash of styles and vintages. Two couches; one leather, one suede. A velour chair with an ottoman and a glass coffee table that looked like it was out of the turn of the millennium. No plants, no pictures, no knick-knacks. It looked worse than a rental; it looked sad, unwelcoming, and sterile.

Belle couldn't see this—it was awful.

And why do you care what she thinks? She's simply a client.

Point taken. Still, I think some new furniture may be in the immediate future of the credit card.

Mitch walked into the open concept kitchen with its traditionally styled cherry cabinets and black granite counters and thought the same thing about this room. It was stunning but felt unused and barren. He owned an embarrassingly ancient collection of mixed pots and pans, and the fridge had minimal supplies of wine, cheese, peanut butter and a couple of eggs. The kitchen had come with a gourmet, six-burner stove that still looked untouched. It was his microwave and Swiss coffee machine in the corner that got the workout.

Again, nothing homey in here to suggest that this place was home to someone who loved to cook. But then he hadn't really cooked in a long while. Once he'd left for college, it was Ramen or takeout. Now, fifteen years later, it was pretty much the same, though the takeout was much more gourmet, and he only wolfed down Ramen in an emergency.

The only room downstairs that was perfect was his office, filling the ground floor wing off the kitchen.

He shut off the lights in the hallway, kitchen, and living room, then climbed the broad, curved, wooden staircase to his bedroom. Quickly brushing his teeth and setting the alarm for 6 a.m., only a few hours from now, he slipped between the king bed's soft sheets and stared at the snow falling outside his window.

Every time he dozed, he awoke suddenly, gripped in a dream where Belle was rejecting every single idea he presented. She was gracious and her smile removed the sting of rejection, but nevertheless, he couldn't help her out of her mess.

Just as Lauren wouldn't allow him to save her life until it was too late to do so, in his nightmare Belle wasn't allowing him to save her nonprofit from Armstrong Worth's silk threads.

4
_____

SHOWERED, WITH HER HAIR AND MAKEUP DONE, INCLUDING an extra layer of concealer she'd used to hide her sleepless night, Belle waited in the living room of the cabin for Mitchell. She'd realized last night that for Armie and her papa to assume that she'd agree to be only the face of her nonprofit was an insult.

In fact she wasn't the face at all. It was the tens of thousands of women who couldn't read well enough to get a job or read the label on a medicine bottle to give their child the correct dosage.

Those women and her mama were the only reason she started Goal 100%. It wasn't a vanity trip at all. It was all about those who needed her nonprofit. Period.

The loud rap on the front door startled her even though she was waiting for it. Belle pulled the door open wide to find Mitchell covered in snow, grasping a travel mug she hoped held coffee. Black, or with cream and sugar...none of that mattered, only that he brought coffee.

And that he was here.

He handed her the mug and stepped backward to shake off his dark woolen hat.

"Where'd you get all that snow?" It was still snowing, but not enough to cover the shoulders of his coat and hat with as much as was piled on at that moment in the short distance from car to cabin.

He pointed upward at the slope of the entryway overhang. She stepped out and looked up. The roof was metal and now practically clear of the white stuff.

"You mean..."

He didn't seem mad, just amused by the situation. That was nice.

Most of the men Belle knew wouldn't have been so accepting of the situation, and somehow it would have been her fault that it happened.

"Yup, so give me a moment to brush off. Then if you're ready, we can head to the office."

Belle sipped from her mug as she watched Mitch dust off his dark blue parka and pull his hat back on.

"Let me get my satchel and we're off. Thanks for the coffee. You have no idea how much that means."

"Oh, but I do. I'm a bit of an addict myself. I remembered Maisie said you were also."

She couldn't believe he'd remembered and been so considerate. Belle shouldered her satchel and locked the door behind her.

"Watch your step. It's icy after we trampled it down last night. When we get back, I'll look for a snow shovel and see about cutting a path."

Just as he finished his warning, Belle slipped and flailed her arms to catch herself. The mug went flying into a snow bank. The dismay on Mitchell's face was so funny that instead of being angry with herself over her clumsiness, she couldn't hold back the laughter. "Your face is priceless."

"Only because now you're going to want to drink mine," he said with a smile.

"Nope, I'm not leaving a great mug of coffee to freeze in the snow." She handed him her satchel and pushed her way through the knee high snow to the divot in the whiteness that showed her where the mug landed, then sunk. Belle fished around for a second and with a great show of triumph held it high. "Good thing this mug self-seals, so your coffee is safe from plunder."

Plunder? Her lips on his cup? Mitch pushed that thought away as quickly as it bloomed in him head. This was dangerous ground his mind was prancing over.

Belle handed him her mug. This time she was the one to dust off the snow that clung to snug, faded jeans tucked into her black leather boots on legs that seemed endless.

His gaze lifted to her face where falling snow clung to her lashes and her sleek cap of auburn hair.

Damn if he didn't want to dust her off himself, then pick her back up and head into the cabin. Screw work.

Mitch shook his head. Enough. It was time to get into his car and head to downtown Boulder and work.

In minutes they were heading down snowy Ninth Street.

"Boulder in summer is gorgeous, but in the winter, it's magical."

He turned to look at her, snuggled into her seat, the mug hovering just below her mouth, held in two hands. Her eyes bright as they took in the mounds of snow on every roof top as they slowly headed down the steep and narrow street.

"This time of year, the Pearl Street Mall is lit up in the evening."

"That would be fun to see. Let's go one night." Belle turned toward him. "Oh. It just dawned on me that I don't know how long I'm going to stay. How many days were you planning to stay in Pagosa Springs?"

Mitch slowed down before his turn onto Walnut Street to see a policewoman blocking the road, signaling him to move on.

He looked past her to see several firetrucks surrounding the building that held the offices of the Icarus Suites.

"Three days tops," he said, distracted as he rolled down the window to speak to the policewoman. "What's going on?"

"Sir, please move on." She pointed for him to continue down Ninth Street.

"But that's my office."

Belle leaned across him to look, and he heard her sharp gasp. "That doesn't look good."

"Hell no, it doesn't."

"Mitch! Mitch!"

He looked toward the voice just as the policewoman was approaching his car, impatient that he was blocking traffic. Denise, the owner of the building was running down the street in sweats and a parka. Waving her arms.

Mitch rolled the down the window and leaned out. "Denise, get in the car. It's cold out there," he yelled.

She jumped in the back. Mitch turned at the next corner, then pulled over to the first open parking spot. It all took less than a minute.

"I tried to text you," Denise said, her voice ragged, her breathing hard.

Both Mitch and Belle turned in their seats to face her.

"Whoa, slow down, Denise. Catch your breath first."

"I don't have time," she said on what was close to a wail.

"What happened?" he asked gently, trying to calm her down.

"I don't know yet. About 5 a.m. I got the call from the alarm company that the sprinklers had gone off, and by the time I got there, a flood was pouring out the doors while the water was beginning to freeze inside. The firemen think the sprinklers where triggered by something on another floor."

Mitch watched as Belle reached over the seat to touch Denise's hand. "I'm Belle Grantham, one of Mitch's clients. What can we do to help?"

Denise gave her a tremulous smile. "That's sweet of you to ask, but I'm afraid there's nothing to be done until the building is declared safe to enter. Then we'll see. I've got insurance, and the Icarus Suites have insurance. I'll be fine, but I worry about my clients at Icarus."

"Can we get you anything—breakfast, coffee?"

"Thanks, Mitch. But Gerald,"—she looked at Belle, sharing the information—"my husband, is here. I'm making his Chevy Tahoe my command center. I got in touch with everyone but you. And I was worried for you, especially after I got your message about coming in first thing."

"No worries about us, but you're sure we can't help?"

"I'll be okay, but thanks again. I'll let you know when we're back up and running. I'm so sorry." Denise opened the door and got out of Mitch's SUV.

He craned his neck and watched her as she walked back the half block to the building. Mitch turned back and faced the windshield, feeling once again that sense of things happening he couldn't control.

One thing after another, starting with Cole and Annie falling in love.

No, be honest with yourself. It started with Lauren's death.

He'd been the one from about the age of ten to make sure they had food on the table. Sometimes it was as simple as scrambled eggs or cold cereal. Other times he'd bring home leftovers from the restaurant where he'd started as a dishwasher and graduated to late-night bartender. Being a waiter didn't work, because he needed to be home to check on Lauren and make sure she ate, did her homework, and went to bed.

He'd wanted to play ice hockey in high school, and Cole helped him get on the team. His scholarship to

Radford was one of the best things that happened. It put him on a path where he excelled and could call his own shots.

Except when he couldn't. Couldn't make his parents love him. Couldn't save Lauren, and now, on a lesser but still important scale, he couldn't present himself and the website to Belle in the manner he thought was important to his business. *And you.*

There was little choice in new venues; it was going to have to be at his home. If he'd only checked his cell phone this morning as was his usual practice, then he'd have been prepared.

"Mitch?" Belle asked.

He turned in his seat to look at her.

"It doesn't sound good about your office. Water and computers don't mix."

The concern in her voice was genuine. She was worried about him, not her presentation.

"I don't keep anything there, it's a conference room only. I just use it for presentations. My office is at my house."

The relief on her face warmed his heart

"I don't care where your office is, it could be on the moon. I'm just glad you didn't lose all your work. For me and for your other clients' sake."

5

THE COMPUTER SCREEN WENT DARK, AND BELLE SAT BACK IN her chair letting the images replay in her head. Mitchell had done a stellar job capturing, in bold and stunning images, her comments from the contest entry.

Tears flooded her eyes. "Mama would have loved this. The image you made of a mother not being able to read the dosing directions on her child's medicine was heartbreaking and terrifying. And the woman who looked so professional and yet couldn't read the menu, hiding her fear that she'd be found out and ostracized...both of those were Mama."

She saw realization and compassion fill Mitchell's blue eyes. "Your mama was illiterate."

"Yes, functionally illiterate. She had dyslexia. She was able to hide it with all sorts of what she called tricks. She said she was filled with shame and exhausted from the effort of hiding it and the ever-present fear of being caught. One day when Papa and she were on a date night,

Papa took her to a new restaurant and told her to pick for both of them. She took a long time reading the menu and told me she was looking for words that were familiar. Finally she put the menu down and asked what the specials of the day were.

"On the way back home Papa pulled the car into their favorite spot on the ranch, on the bluff overlooking Trickle Creek. She told me that he grasped her hand, held it tight, and asked her if there was something she wanted to tell him. And it all spewed out.

"He found the right tutors, and she learned how to compensate for the dyslexia and read. Mama was incredibly smart. She realized there were a few women on the ranch who couldn't read, and she started working with them. Then she created her tutoring method."

"What you use is your mother's method? It's clean, simple, and works. When I called a couple of the Goal 100% programs you've set up—"

"You called them?"

"Sure. I chose you and Goal 100% because my sister, Lauren, and I have always been advocates of literacy. I wanted to know just what you did and if it was working. It is and I wanted to see you succeed. Lauren would have been right in there with you."

"Would have been?"

Belle noticed he looked away and his Adam's apple bobbed a couple of times before he turned back to her. "She died a little over three years ago."

"Oh, Mitchell, I'm so very sorry. It's so hard to lose someone you love."

Belle grabbed his hand and squeezed hard. She felt his fingers wrap around hers and hold. It felt like a hug, warm and comforting.

"You found the exact right tone for my website. Is this why you're so successful?"

Mitchell's fingers tightened on hers for a second and then released. "It's why I ask the questions I ask. Images move people more than simply asking for donations, but you want them to be real, not sappy heart-string pulls."

He was right. His images hit enough of the emotional cues without being sickeningly sentimental.

"Are you ready to see the next stage where I've added the narrative? Then we'll move on to the complete pages where I've asked people for their contributions, the stats of Goal 100% that you gave me, and the mission statement. Then you can tell if it still hits the right chord."

The entire process fascinated Belle. It was like creating a super short movie, carrying you through the story and then the conclusion. Once again she realized she was so lucky to have Mitchell working for her.

Working with her, she amended hastily.

"Yes, I'm ready. I don't want to stop now."

MITCH WATCHED BELLE'S FACE AS THE FINAL PAGE PLAYED one last time. He'd added more information to each subsequent version he'd shown her so she could comment if she wanted. And lastly the final page with its plea to donate.

Belle wasn't just watching, she was absorbing and analyzing.

His clients usually looked and nodded or shook their heads. Less than half offered suggestions to explain the head shake, so Mitch had to guess, and tried to pull information from them. It would be interesting to see what Belle said.

He let the last image fade, waited a moment as he always did when he was presenting his final image for each web page in the project's site, then got up from his chair and turned on his office lights.

Belle squinted in the bright lights.

"So that's the tone I'm hoping will pull your donors in. There are a few more pages we'll want to add as more centers are created," Mitch said in his best no-nonsense business voice. "And when this is right, I've booked a studio session with real models instead of the stock images I used here. And maybe even a bit of video from one of your centers."

This was the moment. He hoped she liked most of it, since the first images struck a chord in her. But if not, he'd continue until she was completely happy with it. She needed this as a nuclear-grade weapon in her armory so she could fight her board, who wanted to take so much away from her.

"If I said it was perfect, would you get a swelled head and be impossible?" Belle tilted her head and gazed up at him.

"Yes," he answered cautiously. Her green eyes were lit with merriment. What was she up to?

"Then I guess I'll have to find something that needs to be fixed in order to puncture that swelled head."

Mitch held his grin back, sat down and swiveled his chair to face her. He crossed his arms over his chest. "Shoot," he said, tone serious.

"I didn't like the exclamation point at the end of Volunteer to Be a Tutor and Change a Future. It needs to be a simple period."

"Okay, and ...?"

"That's it. Let's have a celebratory lunch, and then we can go over anything you think needs more punch. I want to get this puppy live and working for me and show Armie that he can donate, and that I don't need *his* 'talent' to make Goal 100% healthy and strong."

Mitch knew she most likely did need help, but not to the extreme Armstrong Worth was proposing.

"I don't think I have anything in the fridge we can eat, so we can head over to the grocery store or hit a restaurant."

He'd been amazed she'd not turned up her nose at his lack of furnishings, or the fact that his office was designed as a working space and not stylish or sleek.

"No worries, I can tell this is a bachelor's pad."

Uh oh. Maybe he'd been totally wrong. "Yeah, there is a definite lack of furniture—"

"Or pictures and stuff. It's like every other single man's house I've seen, with the exception of Armie, who had a designer 'do' his."

Belle quoted "do" in the air with her fingers and Mitch felt the sudden tightness loosen in the back of his neck.

"And frankly I think Armie's place is a bit sterile. You'll get around to fixing it up sooner or later. Instead of lunch out, let's go to the market. The snow is still falling, but if the store is close and your fancy SUV will make it, I need fresh air before we tackle the next steps, and I'll need some supplies for the cabin."

Mitch fixed the exclamation point, sliding his gaze to Belle and seeing her grin grow wider. Then he backed up the work three times on three different sources and rose from the chair, stretching backward with his arms laced over his head.

He glanced over at Belle to see her gaze centered on his bare stomach above the waistband of his jeans where his shirt had pulled free.

6

MITCH WATCHED HER FACE UNTIL HER GAZE SLOWLY LIFTED to meet his. The devil in him overrode his good sense, and he raised one brow as if saying, "like what you see?"

He didn't expect red to flood her face as she looked away immediately.

"Lunch. We need, uh, lunch," Belle said in a strangled voice.

Laughter rolled up from deep in his soul and rumbled out. It felt good to have his workouts appreciated. He didn't have six-pack abs, but close. He worked weights with Cole and Brice Young, a minimum of three times a week. Sweating and grunting was a great stress reducer, and all three of them had needed it, with the double wedding coming up. Or so said Cole and Brice.

Mitch didn't think the two grooms looked like they needed any help with stress, but he knew he sure as hell did.

But since yesterday and meeting Belle, he'd laughed more than he had in the entire year. And damn it felt good.

Then the face of Lauren swam into his consciousness, and the guilt he always felt the moment a bit of happiness flooded into his life surfaced. His laughter choked off and the silence in the room was thick.

He'd wondered more than one sleepless night whether or not his nephews were moving away from him. If Annie was supplanting their mother's place. If Lauren's laugh had faded from their memory.

He had videos of all of them together before Lauren got sick and once in a while he'd play them for the boys. Josh still laughed at them, but it seemed Peter was less interested these days. And that hurt Mitch.

"I'm sorry."

Mitch blinked and turned his attention to the simply gorgeous woman in front of him. A frown wrinkled her brow and worry filled her hazel eyes.

"For what?"

"For acting like a silly girl and blushing over a bit of skin. Embarrassing you."

He couldn't let her think it was that. He'd loved the spontaneity of the moment. "It wasn't that at all."

"Then why the sudden pain in your eyes."

Mitch didn't share emotions this deep with anyone, even the lovely, worried lady in front of him. His grief counselor said he should try and share, that it would help him cope with the guilt. That he wasn't the only one to have something like this cloud their life. But he didn't even know where to start, so he didn't.

"My turn to apologize. I shouldn't have teased you."

"I'm used to teasing and I always blush, so I'm giving you fair warning."

"Duly noted."

His stomach decided to intervene and let loose a huge rumble.

"Let's feed that beast," Belle said with a smile.

A merry twinkle now replaced the worry in her eyes. Mitch couldn't help his lips curve upward in return. He checked his watch. "It's far later than I thought."

BELLE PUSHED AWAY HER WORRY OVER MITCH'S SUDDEN change of mood. She'd been pretty sure it wasn't her blush that caused it and figured he'd tell her when he was ready ... or he wouldn't.

They left his house and to her amazement turned west to head up Baseline Road. "I don't remember a food store near here."

"Nope, there isn't one. But I thought we could wait another couple of minutes until I checked on Cole's house. I promised to look at it daily. Do you mind?"

"No, of course not."

They turned down a street near the entrance to Chautauqua Park and Belle gasped. In the deepening dusk a house shone with what must be a million lights. "Hooboy, I wouldn't want that electric bill."

"Annie would probably agree, but it's her tradition."

"Annie? Who is that?"

"Annabelle Hamilton, author of the Star Light, Star Bright children's books. She's Cole's new wife. They're in Hawaii on their honeymoon with my nephews." Mitch turned into a driveway and parked the car.

"Really? I've heard of her." Belle twisted in her seat. "Is this your Cole's house?"

"Yes."

"You mean Cole and Annie lived next door to each other and now they're married?"

"Yes again."

Belle waited for more explanation, but Mitch got out of the SUV and came around to open her door.

"Hey, Mitch."

Belle looked toward the voice to see the most perfect couple in the world standing next to an SUV in the driveway. "Didn't you also say they were in Hawaii," she asked Mitch.

"Yep. That's Annie's best friend, Jennifer, and her new husband, Brice. It was a double wedding on Saturday."

Jennifer and Brice headed in their direction. "Mitch, what are you doing in town? I thought you had a client in Pagosa Springs," the tall man questioned.

"Meet my client, Belle Grantham."

As she had in the airport, Belle felt Mitch's hand on her lower back and again enjoyed his protective touch.

Belle held out her hand. Jennifer grasped it firmly.

"Jennifer Malloy and Brice Young" she introduced.

"Or Jennifer Malloy-Young and Brice Young," Brice said, shaking his head and sighing dramatically. "I don't think my new wife has fully realized we're married."

Belle saw Jennifer grin at Brice's teasing and liked the couple immediately.

"We're just making good on our promise to check Annie's house and make sure the lights are okay. And Brice just finished snowplowing duty, then we're going home to do ours. Hey, we're grilling tonight—"

"In this weather?"

"Nothing stops a Young from grilling." Brice added.

"And we got a shipment of greens from Brice's sister, who belongs to a food co-op that their dad manages. Want to come over for dinner?"

Belle very much wanted to and put as much affirmative as she could into her gaze when she looked at Mitch.

"Yes. But I warn you, we're starving and we're heading to the market right after this."

"Can we stop and get some wine or anything for dessert?" Belle asked, so pleased that he wanted to go. And it would be good for her to be in company, diluting the spell cast by Mitch.

He was smart, compassionate, a gentleman—and he laughed. A good hearty laugh.

"We have a lot of wine left from the wedding, and I'm making a special dessert, so I think we're set. Do you know the way to the house, Mitch?" Jen asked.

"I was there recently with Brice when you were in DC on a trip. He wanted me to test a new gadget."

"Right, and it worked, didn't it?" Brice said.

"First time," Mitch agreed.

Jennifer just rolled her eyes. "That's my love, always has a new gadget. So we'll see you in a bit?"

Belle again looked at Mitch, and they nodded in unison.

The couple headed down the freshly plowed sidewalk, and Belle realized the entire block was plowed and the other side as well.

"He did all that?" She swept her arm to encompass the block.

"I'm guessing he did. Annie usually does it all, so he's probably keeping up her tradition."

"Your Annie sounds like something."

"Cole's Annie."

In that instant Belle understood Mitch a bit better. It didn't sound as if he disliked the woman who took his deceased sister's place, but he seemed to have not fully accepted her place in his family tree.

7

WINE GLASS IN HAND, BELLE STOOD AT THE WALL OF windows facing south in Jennifer's house high on a bluff, giving an unparalleled view of Boulder below. The snow continued to fall, then suddenly it tapered and stopped. The clouds began to lift off the foothills, revealing the Flatirons.

Belle vividly remembered her first sight of Boulder and its massive, iconic up-tilted slabs of sandstone that fronted the mountains.

Her papa, driving the family up from Texas on their way to Estes Park, pulled into the Davidson Mesa turnoff just before the ribbon of highway dropped steeply into the valley that held Boulder.

They were a family of four: Mama was still alive, and Belle was starting high school, while Junior was a senior. Life was carefree.

She felt Mitch join her at the huge picture window. The man had a spark that set a tingle alive inside her.

Something she'd not felt before. And goodness knows she'd dated more frequently than any of her friends. Or at least *had* dated. Now she was simply too busy.

Most of your friends are married by now.

That thought jolted her and she pushed it to the back of her mind.

"Jennifer says dinner will be ready in a few minutes," Mitch said softly. "That's a pretty amazing view of the Flatirons, isn't it?"

"It really is. I've loved those since I first saw them. They seem like a backbone to the city. But what is that star on the side of the mountain?"

"That's Flagstaff Mountain, and the star is only lit in winter. Annie thinks it means hope and peace, celebrating the season."

"What does it mean to you?"

Mitch turned to look at her, and his electric blue eyes dimmed a bit. "I don't know," he shrugged. "It's just a manmade star to me."

"Hmmm, I think it's more. It's so peaceful and yet beckoning. I'll let the image sit and see what I think it means."

"Dinner is ready, if you guys are," Brice said from behind them.

Belle startled. She hadn't heard him come into the room, so focused was she on the scene in front of her and the man beside her. And the pain that seemed to run to his very core. She wished she could help him. Find a way to soothe it, or at best, eradicate the source.

Maybe he'd confide in her someday.

She turned to Brice and sniffed the air. "Wow, it smells delicious. And I like your apron. 'Grill Master.'" She read the bold type aloud.

"That's me. And the wine opener."

"Expert at both." Jennifer came up behind him and laced her arms around his middle and hugged. Then she released him and gestured to the table, already set with candles burning. When did they do that? Had she really been that absorbed in memories, then in Mitch? "Can I help bring out anything? I've not done much except drink wine and enjoy your home."

"Nope, I've got my waitstaff right here." Jennifer nodded toward Brice.

"Where would you like me to sit?"

Jennifer nodded to Mitch, who had already pulled back a chair. "He's giving you the view. He's always surprising me," she added softly, leaning toward Belle so Mitch couldn't hear.

Belle couldn't help but smile at Jennifer's whisper. Too bad she didn't live closer. Belle thought the woman would be a great friend.

Jennifer left for the kitchen and came back quickly, placing a platter of grilled flank steak on the center of the table. By the scent wafting up from the festive plate, Belle thought it had been marinated in something wonderful.

A moment later, Jennifer brought back a baking dish of perfectly browned scalloped potatoes while Brice carried in a huge bowl of Caesar salad. He poured the Cabernet and sat at one end of the table with Jennifer at the other.

For a few moments nobody said a thing as they passed

the food around. "These potatoes look heavenly," Belle said as she put a hearty spoonful of the creamy casserole on her plate.

"Jen has my blue ribbon for these, and Annie makes the best mashed potatoes I've ever tasted," Brice said.

"I make a mean Texas twice-baked potato—it was my mama's favorite side dish."

Jennifer tipped her head in question, and Belle oddly felt safe enough with these three people to explain her use of *was* when talking about her mama. "She died ten years ago, T-boned in Austin." Safe or not, the sadness still made her throat tighten up. She sipped her wine, hoping it would help loosen the knot. "It's her teaching method that I use for the Goal 100% ~ Literacy for Women programs."

"So the website Mitch is working on is for literacy?" Jennifer asked. "Tell us more about it."

Belle knew her face beamed. This was her baby and she never tired of talking about it.

"Yes, it was a godsend to win Mitch's contest. And I warn you I can get long-winded talking about my passion, so stop me if I do."

She took another sip of wine to wet her throat. "While I want to promote literacy for all, my focus right now, with my limited funding, is primarily literacy for women. They can then help their kids with homework, etcetera, and then teach other family members to read. And if I'm lucky, they'll want to become a volunteer with the program and pay it forward."

Jennifer nodded and a gleam lit her eyes. "Are your centers staffed by volunteers?"

"Completely. And the space is donated. The sessions are held at a library, a church hall, or a community center. Sometimes even at the recipient's home. Goal 100% provides the materials, the training, and the ongoing support. I travel a lot, and I'd like to have paid regional staffers to do the training, the facilitating.

"But that takes a lot more money than I currently bring in. That's where Mitchell comes in. His website design is..." Belle thought for a second, needing to find the right words. Then she smiled. "Astonishing. You take a journey as you click through the pages."

Belle noticed a different look in Jennifer's eyes as she looked in Mitch's direction. Respect and curiosity.

"Always surprising me," Jennifer murmured, again so only Belle could hear her.

"So there you have it." Belle was absolutely starving, but instead of tucking into the delicious food, held up her wine glass. "To Jennifer and Brice—thank you for this incredible meal and congratulations on your marriage. I hope you both live long and prosper."

She winced as the sentence came out, but Brice grinned. "A fellow Trekkie is among us, meaning of course, we're going to be lifelong friends."

"Shatner, Stewart, or Mulgrew?" Mitch asked Brice. "Which of those is your favorite *Star Trek* captain?"

"Wait, you left out a bunch more. There's—"Jennifer protested.

"Nope. Gotta pick one out of those three," Mitch countered.

"Then it's got to be Shatner," Brice said.

"Mulgrew," Belle countered quickly.

"Stewart." Jennifer sighed.

"Shatner," Mitch said. "But there is only one Spock, sorry to all the rest of the Spocks out there, but Nimoy was the best." He held up his glass in a toast to the first and best sidekick in the original *Star Trek*.

Belle quickly raised hers as did Jennifer and Brice.

Mitch saw Belle's full-on, bright-green gaze as she laughed with the rest of them. She was so full of life and fun. Belle fit in well with Jennifer and Brice, and they seemed to like her.

Why wouldn't they?

Why do you have to be so damn concerned that she's a rich girl instead of just enjoying her?

They finished the meal talking about the various *Star Trek* movies and which they liked best. Brice mentioned that his sister Caro was going to do a huge, interactive experience at San Diego's Comic-Con this year and would be in Denver next year.

When Jennifer slipped away to bring in her secret dessert, Brice topped off their wine glasses, then cleared the dinner plates, refusing help from either of them.

"They're really nice, Mitchell. You're lucky to have such good friends."

It surprised him that Belle thought they were friends. Yes, on one level they were, but they'd rarely shared confidences, and Mitch had only been to this amazing house once. Whereas Jennifer, Brice, Annie, and Cole got together all the time.

And whose fault is that? You were asked and after refusing enough times, the invites dwindled.

But in a flash, Mitch wanted this. He enjoyed laughing and even being a bit silly. It just hadn't happened with any regularity in a long while. He'd been happy in high school playing ice hockey with Cole. When Lauren got old enough for Cole to notice her as a woman rather than a younger sister tag-along, life was still fun if not as simple.

He'd admit he was happiest in college when a whole new world opened up to him in web design.

Cole and Lauren married and, as expected, started their own lives and had two wonderful boys. They were in Virginia and he'd moved to Colorado.

He should have looked for a new group of friends, but instead buried himself in first the Web Wizards biz in Denver and then in starting his own in Boulder.

Then Lauren got sick, and his trips to Virginia increased but naturally weren't the same. Nothing was the same.

Now he wanted a bit of liveliness back his life. The same black guilt as always flooded him at that thought, yet this time when he pushed it back, it dimmed. Mitch knew though that when he was alone, the fact that he was alive and Lauren wasn't would haunt his dreams.

But for now, this was real and felt right.

He smiled at Belle across the table. "I think you really should start calling me Mitch. Mitchell is way too formal."

"Mitch it is." Belle's eyes flashed with the prolonged merriment of the evening.

All of a sudden the lights dimmed over the table. They both glanced toward the kitchen to see Jennifer carrying out a tray of white porcelain ramekins with flaming contents.

"Wow, dramatic. What is it?"

"Crème brûlée with lit brandy."

Jennifer placed the tray in the center of the table and the flames died, leaving the sugar topping browned and crisp. "My secret is to brown the sugar ahead of time, then do this flame trick for presentation."

"It worked. I'm going to steal this for my next dinner party."

"Do you give dinner parties often?" Mitch asked, intrigued that she too liked cooking.

"Not since I left Texas. But I always enjoyed them when I did. Sometimes they were intimate like this." Belle swept her hand around the table. "Other times we'd have 100-plus people for a Texas barbecue."

"Now that sounds fun. And I bet the food is finger-licking good."

"You bet. No napkins allowed at a barbecue."

"Hey, we're having a trim-the-tree party later this week —do you both want to come?"

Mitch felt Belle's gaze and waited for her answer. It sounded fun. As long as she came with him.

"I don't know if I'll still be in town. Mitchell, er, Mitch, had planned only three days' work, so we might be done by Tuesday. I have to get back to Pagosa Springs on

Thursday, the twenty-third. I've got Papa and my brother coming in for Christmas. But if I'm still here, I'd love to come. That is, if Mitch will tag along?"

"Sure, it would be fun. Thanks."

"I'M SORRY WE NEVER MADE IT TO THE MARKET, BUT AT least Jen and Brice gave you some coffee, creamer, and sugar," Mitch said as he pulled in front of her cabin, parked, and turned toward her. It was late, past 11 p.m., and they were both tired.

And energized, at least he was. It had been a fun evening. The best in a long, long time.

"Don't forget the bagels and cream cheese, fruit, and a bottle of that great wine Jen sent home with me. With that I'm set. So tomorrow we can have breakfast here and then head to your computer."

"Thanks, sounds great. So I'll see you around what, eight-thirty?"

"That's a good time. Not too early, not too late, just right."

"A Goldilocks and a *Star Trek* fan?"

"Yep, I loved that story—it was so cute. I wanted to be blonde for the longest time."

"Your hair suits you. It's perfect."

Her eyes widened and she leaned forward.

Before he knew it, Belle had brushed his lips in a kiss, then leaned back in her seat.

"Thank you. For everything. What you've done has been far beyond what I dreamt could be done."

Mitch was still bemused from the swift warmth of her lips on his.

He blinked and focused. "Belle, you and your nonprofit are worth fighting for."

Did that really just leave my lips?

Then the happiness in her gaze made him realize that the core of Belle was to help, to nurture, to give.

He be damned if Worth and Papa Grantham would take this away from her.

He shifted and started to open his door.

"Don't get out. I can make it to the door."

"And I was going to shovel it today for you. Tomorrow's job. I'll wait until you're inside, okay?"

"Deal. Sweet dreams."

"You, too."

8

BELLE CLOSED THE CABIN DOOR BEHIND HER AND LEANED against it. She was surprised at the intensity of the need that flooded her when she kissed Mitch. Maybe it wasn't the smartest thing for her to do, but what he'd given her today went straight to her heart.

And darn if he wasn't a hunk in the best possible way. Those blue eyes that changed from electric to piercing in a moment. That chin that brooked no nonsense. And those lips that, when curved in a smile, melted her because it was a real grin.

She'd seen her fill of good-looking men, and frankly most were unapproachable or too darn vain to be interesting.

Mitch was neither of those. In fact she'd be surprised if he thought of himself as handsome.

Her cell phone rang, an unwelcome intrusion to her delicious day dreaming. She quickly put her care packages on the couch and pulled out her cell phone. She looked at caller ID, intending to refuse the call until she saw the name. "Armie, what a surprise."

"Really? You were pretty riled up when I left you the other night."

"I was and still am, so beware. The good news is that the web pages are looking really good. Mitch has the tone of what Goal 100% is down perfectly."

"I told you he was a genius. And I'm guessing since you're still a bit mad, you haven't yet come to the realization that my proposal makes sense."

"Sense? Armie, you, all three of you, are asking too much and giving me too little time. Give me at least another year using my trust for helping with the bills and seeing where I go with the website. Instead of fighting me or threatening me, add in your donation and use your name to promote the nonprofit," she suggested.

"Belle, it's ..."

"It will buy me time. I'm not failing at this. Simple. Your plan takes too much away from me. I just wish you, Papa, and Junior would believe in this as strongly as I do. See it the way Mitch saw it the first time he read my contest entry. He got it."

"You're in over your head, Belle."

"I'm not. I picked you three for my board because I thought you'd be on the side of my cause. Not the side of money."

Silence was her answer, but the connection hadn't been lost, and Belle realized she'd played her hand too heavily.

"Gotta run, breakfast is over. The meetings are finished

tomorrow evening, so I'll be back in the States Wednesday before dawn. When I get to the office, I'll call. We can talk more then."

"Armie, we don't need to talk. I've—" But now she was talking to a dead line.

Damn him. Why did he have to make her a deal that would take away the essence of her nonprofit? Why not simply make a donation? She *was* tired to the bone, but she was also strong, and a little more exhaustion wasn't going to kill her.

Belle glanced at the clock and saw it was near 1 a.m. She was too agitated to sleep and decided a fire was what she needed. Logs had already been stacked in the river-stone-faced fireplace, and there was a box of fatwood nearby. She found matches and lit the tinder, watching it catch the split logs.

She opened the bottle of wine Jennifer had sent and watched as the flames burned bright and hot.

And she wanted Mitch there. Beside her, to talk in positive terms about the website, the nonprofit.

It was odd that a man she'd just met understood this need better than those she'd spent her whole life around. Mitch was a self-made man as were Armie and Papa. Even Junior was working on a pet project.

Working hard was part of the deal. Mama had worked hard running the ranch alongside Papa and, added to that, she had her literacy work, her cause. Belle had simply picked up that banner and was still running with it.

Goal 100% ~ Literacy for Women wasn't going to

bankrupt her or hurt her, so why was her board so adamant she give it up?

WITH A GLOVED FIST MITCH KNOCKED AGAIN ON THE CABIN'S wood door. The morning was overcast with heavy snow clouds and dim natural light. It was easy to see there were no lights on in the cabin.

He checked his watch again, eight-thirty on the dot.

Mitch pulled off the glove on his right hand, thinking the glove had muffled the sound. As he raised his fist to knock a third time, Belle opened the door, clad in an oversized, white terry robe long enough to sweep the floor with its hem. Belle's usual sleek cap of auburn hair was tangled on her left side, and her eyes were still heavy with sleep.

It took all his will power not to drop his jaw in surprise. "Late night?"

"I'm so sorry I overslept. I had a phone call from Armie... Shoot, come in, I'm sorry. I'll get the coffee started, and we can talk after my first sip." She closed the door behind him after he'd entered.

He saw the ashes in the fireplace and the bottle of wine on the coffee table. She must have been up far later than he. He'd crashed but had woken realizing he'd been dreaming of her. He was hard, taut with desire, and wanting Belle with a ferociousness that stunned him. Nothing like this had happened since college.

Those dreams had been pretty erotic. Her kiss last

night, while nearly chaste, had awakened his body from its near monastic state.

Having her appear sleepy and tousled in front of him resurrected those images from his dream. And started his body reacting as well.

"How about I'll get the coffee started, and you go do whatever you need to do."

"Really? You're not mad?"

He turned from taking off his coat and hat.

"Mad? Why would I be?"

"Because you seem to like being on a schedule."

Mitch blinked. Schedule? Really, is that how he came across? "Go, I'll be in the kitchen. And no worries about me being mad or anything, 'K?"

She ran out of the living room toward the bedroom.

Sheesh, she didn't have to run.

And schedule? Mad? He wondered about Belle's words as he put the grounds in the paper filter and filled the coffeemaker's tank with water. Maybe he was still a grouch. Annie had called him that. Cole called him worse, and sometimes the boys looked at him like he'd sprouted horns.

When had he lost the simple joy of being alive? The pleasure of making sure that the needs of the people around him were met?

Mitch shook his head, and glanced in the direction Belle had fled.

Damn.

Yes, he was always on a schedule and had been since he was a boy. That's the way he made it all work. And for the immediate future, he didn't see a way to change that as far as his business.

What he needed to add to his life was a bit more spontaneity, more flexibility. Last night had been a good start.

Mitch yawned—courtesy of those dreams last night— as he poked his head into the fridge and found a couple of bagels, a few eggs, and some cheese, courtesy of the care package Jen had sent home with Belle last night.

"Hey," he called. "Do you want breakfast in?"

"Honestly? That'd be great. Then we can go to your office," she said from behind him.

He jumped, hitting his head on the refrigerator shelf. "Ouch! You scared me," he mumbled as he backed out of the refrigerator and looked at her.

A slight smile curved her lips, then disappeared. "Are you hurt?"

"No." He rubbed the sore spot on the back of his head. "But you must move like a cat. I didn't hear you come in."

"Ballet training." Belle raised her hands over her head in a graceful arc and moved her feet into some complicated stance. "Fifth position."

"No kidding?"

"Nope, I thought I'd be good at it, but honestly, I was too tall. I was no swan, more of a goose."

"You look pretty much like a swan to me." Earning another smile from Belle.

In fact he was envious that she could look so refreshed. She'd shed her tiredness faster than he had. At the moment she wore tight black pants—he thought they were called leggings—and an ivory sweater that came to her thighs. Damn if she didn't look like a million bucks. And everything she had on probably cost a pretty penny.

God, why can't you get past her rich heritage? It's not her fault she was born with a silver spoon in her mouth.

Her smile faltered and he realized he was frowning. He wasn't about to crush her moment just because he was a jerk. "Can you do one of those twirly moves?"

"A pirouette? Sure, no toe shoes, but socks on the wood floor will help."

And sure enough she spun, then slipped, and he caught her. Both of them tumbling to the floor with Belle landing on top of him, knocking the air right out of him.

He rose with effort and leaned on his elbow, trying to catch his breath.

"Mitch, did I hurt you?"

He held up one hand, signaling he needed a moment. It did hurt. Then the image played in his mind of her twirling around so gracefully, but ending on the floor in a heap.

The first sound out of his mouth was laughter. Which she echoed as they lay in a tangle on the kitchen floor.

And damn if this didn't feel natural. No barrier, no artifice, just a funny circumstance they shared.

BELLE PUSHED BACK FROM THE TABLE, HER BELLY FULL OF several cups of coffee and the omelet Mitch had whipped up.

"After this I really need a walk. Do we have time?"

"Sure, there's nothing much left to do on the website, since you're such an easy client."

Belle wrinkled her nose at him. "Because you read my mind and created everything I dreamt of."

"Okay, so we have a mutual admiration society going on. Cool. Anyway, I don't have the photo shoot set up until tomorrow afternoon, and I could use the exercise as well."

Mitch grabbed the dishes and headed toward the sink. That stunned her. Then she remembered he was a bachelor and if he didn't do the dishes, there wasn't anyone else to do them. Unless he had staff, and after seeing his house yesterday, she was fairly sure a cleaning service wasn't necessary. There was nothing to dust.

"Wait, you said photo shoot?"

Water ran into the sink and she got up from the table to take over cleanup duty.

"I can do dishes, you know," he said.

"I know, so I'll dry, okay?" After pulling open several drawers to no avail, she found the dish towels and grabbed one, placing it over her arm. Ready to do drying duty. "About the photo shoot," she prodded him.

"Remember when I said we'd have the real pictures once we'd nailed the tone and direction you wanted to go? Well, I would have been back in Boulder by tomorrow afternoon, so I set it up before I left."

"Do you think I could come along? Would it bother you?"

"Sure you can, but I thought maybe you wanted or needed to head back to Pagosa Springs."

"No, like I said last night, I don't need to go back until the twenty-third, or very early the twenty-fourth."

She didn't want to head back. It wasn't as if she were lonely, she had friends and of course her work. But after last night's call from Armie, she couldn't sleep, and a few ah-ha moments had hit her.

She could, of course, have used Austin, the closest big city near the family ranch, for headquartering her nonprofit, but it was too close.

Too close to family, to Armie, to her circle, the friends she'd grown up with, and their parents.

The second ah-ha moment was that she really liked being around Mitch. He was funny and talented and oh-so fine looking. But there was more to him and she wasn't ready to part ways.

"Anyway nobody will miss me, and the centers are closed for the week. This work"—as her heart screamed *Mitch* in place of *work*—"is too important and too interesting to leave."

"Good. Believe it or not, I wasn't ready for you to head back. This *work* is too interesting to do alone."

Her heart thundered. Did she just hear a subtle play on her words that Mitch was interested in her? Maybe even a tad bit more than interested?

She kept her eyes on the pan she dried and dried again. And cursed the red heat she felt in her cheeks. Finally, she put the pan away, feeling more in control.

Belle and Mitch bundled up in their jackets, hats, and gloves for their walk. It would be good to be outdoors and away from the enticing intimacy of Mitch in the small cabin.

Bluebell Road, one of the main trails up into the park, was steep and crowded. As they reached the top, the road forked, just as she'd remembered. One path headed toward the Enchanted Mesa trail and NCAR, and the other toward the base of those magnificent snow-covered Flatirons and Rainbow Arch. Both were packed with people. Some had snowshoes and poles, and others wore little more than running gear and fleece.

The sun turned the snow into a glittering white blanket and added a lot of unexpected warmth.

"Let's go and sit on that big rock in the sun." She pointed to the middle of the field. "I bet we have a great view of Boulder. And in the sun, I can shed my jacket. It's hot."

Mitch laughed. "That's one of the great things about Colorado. And as you know from Pagosa Springs' elevation, sun at any time of the year will warm you."

They trekked a short distance through the snow and sat on the boulder in silence. The kind that was comfortable, not strained or awkward.

After a couple of minutes, she thought now was a good time to explain what happened that kept her up so late. "So, as I said, Armie called me last night."

Mitch turned from the panorama of the snow-blanketed city below and the mountains to the west to face her. "Was he still trying to convince you to take his deal?"

"Yeah. I was about to tell him my decision and the line went dead." She trailed off, not wanting to say more until she got Mitch's reaction. Why she was waiting for his thoughts confused her, yet, she trusted him.

"Belle, are you asking me for my opinion?"

She nodded and felt a bit of the day's brightness dim under the uncertainty of what he'd say.

"This is your dream. I've said that before. It's yours and those thousands, and eventually millions, of women you'll help by setting up the centers and sessions to tutor them in reading. Imagine the first time they see letters forming a word that makes sense. I can't tell you which way you should go. I can tell you about my decision when I had to make a tough call."

She nodded, eager that Mitch was allowing her a glimpse into him.

"I moved across the country to take a job at Web Wizards. I left my sister, brother-in-law, and two nephews in Virginia to come to Colorado. There were three openings and over a thousand applicants. I got one of the spots—of course I was going to take it. And I loved the job, at first. I made great money, was never bored, but also eventually realized that I was spending my life working for someone else. I was fulfilling their dream, not mine."

Belle put her hand on his thigh. He didn't pull away or remove her hand, thankfully, because she needed this physical connection and hoped it might make him feel the same way.

"So after a bit longer than a year, I turned in my notice and opened my own company. It didn't take long for my clients to realize I wasn't there and find me at my new website. I didn't solicit them. I still liked the folks at Web

Wizards and—I'm blowing my horn here—I knew I'd get clients soon enough. And I did.

"So I guess I'm saying, fight hard for your dream. Not everyone will believe in it, and some will want to talk you out of it. But if you don't go for it, then all you have is stardust."

"So, Mitch, are you happy?"

9

Was he happy? What a loaded question Belle just asked. All Mitch could do was be honest. That was fair to her. "Somewhat."

He glanced at his watch and realized time was passing and they had work to do before the photo shoot tomorrow. Perfect opportunity to change the subject. The day was too perfect to face deeper questions about his answer.

"Time to go. I don't know if any of what I said answered your question about Worth's offer. But honestly, Belle, nobody can tell you what fork you should take."

"That was a bad segue. But you're right."

"I thought it was pretty darn good myself." And with that, he held out a hand to her. They followed their footprints in the deep snow back to Bluebell Road, past the fork, and down to the cabin and his SUV.

The cold tempered by the intense high-altitude sunshine and the beauty of the day continued to brighten his mood. *It's not due simply to Colorado. Give Belle the credit as well. Despite the fact that you may still be uptight over the fact she's from a privileged family, she brings out something better in you.*

Mitch spent the next few hours in his office practically knee to knee with Belle. Getting the last image ideas nailed and the text to reinforce what the viewer saw. And how important support of Goal 100% was to women.

They were making the last bits of the website solid before the shoot tomorrow, so all he had to do was insert the images and maybe make a bit of them into short videos.

However, sitting in this close proximity, watching Belle's lashes sweep her cheek when she blinked, the way she cupped her chin in her palm when she was thinking, the way he felt her sneak peeks at him...it all made it harder—heck, nearly impossible—to concentrate.

Belle would get up and refill their coffee cups from his fancy Swiss coffeemaker, and later in the afternoon, she brought in cheese and crackers on a plate.

"Hey, this is all I could find in the fridge. We'll definitely need to finally get to the market. I'm making you dinner," she said and then yawned hugely. "Sorry. It was a late, late night."

Mitch grinned. "Listen, why don't you stretch out on one of the couches? There's an afghan in the chest next to the TV. Take a nap. I only have about an hour of code work left, then we can head to the store."

She didn't need any coaxing as she practically jumped from the chair and waved him goodbye with the back of her hand.

Mitch munched a few of the crackers as he added another layer of protection to Belle's site. Brice and Jen had developed a couple of protocols for him to add to his clients' sites to help deter hackers. Even so, he advised all his clients to invest in some strong security to scan for threats.

As another layer of support, something he didn't do for his usual clients, he bought a two-year subscription for Belle's site to one of Brice's midrange security packages. Call it a donation to her nonprofit.

He wondered how it would turn out for her in the long run. There were scores of literacy projects around the country vying for the same dollars.

This was a tangible dream of Belle's. Real. She wasn't dabbling at this as a time-filler, she was honoring the memory, passion, and work of her mother. It was a helluva tribute. One that would change lives.

Mitch's eyes felt dry and he blinked, then looked at the computer screen's blinking cursor. Wondering how much time he'd zoned out and shaking his head as he realized it had been minutes, not seconds, he'd been thinking about Belle.

Another twenty minutes of intense work, and he was done until the photo shoot. Once those images were ready, he'd work his own magic with them, make this site live and make her other one disappear in a seamless transition.

Save, save, save to his backup drives and he was done.

Stretching mightily and letting loose his own huge yawn, Mitch left his office in search of Belle.

She wasn't in the living room. Odd. Though there was

a sofa pillow lying flat on the cushions with a head imprint square in the middle of it.

There weren't many other places for her to stretch out. He tiptoed up the wood stairs, vowing to order a carpet runner to dampen the noise of footfalls. He peeked into his room, praying she hadn't decided to use his bed. He wasn't sure he could resist the temptation to snuggle there next to her.

Nope, his bed's duvet wasn't rumpled. *Damn.*

He didn't bother peeking into two of the rooms as they were devoid of furnishings. Then he gently pushed open the door to his nephews' rooms, always ready for them in case of a sleepover.

There, smack in the middle of Josh's double bed, was Belle, curled up under the afghan, sound asleep. Her palm was tucked beneath her cheek. Her breathing was soft and even.

His body reacted instantly.

The afghan was pulled down to her waist, and she had to be cold. The room's thermostat was set low unless the boys used the room, so he turned it up. Then he carefully reached across the bed, grasped the edge of the cover and pulled it up to her shoulders.

BELLE FELT THE WARMTH AND PULL OF THE BLANKET AS IT moved up her shoulders. What a nice guy to worry about her being cold. Briefly opening one eye, she saw Mitch staring at her and let her instinct rule as she reached out and grasped his wrist. "Are you finished with the site?"

"I thought you were asleep."

"I am. My eyes are closed."

"Sleep talking, huh?"

"Good at it."

"Yes, I'm done and was going to grab a power nap since you were having one. Then we'll finally head out to the market for real food."

Belle scooted over to one side, making room for him. "You can nap here, the blanket is big enough for both of us."

She felt his hesitation. Maybe she'd come on too strong. But she was cozy and drowsy, and why shouldn't he enjoy the same? It wasn't as if they weren't fully clothed and on top of the sheets.

Which of course wouldn't matter if the pull of hormones was happening.

Finally she felt the mattress sag a bit on one side and heard his clothes rustle as he stretched out.

"Go ahead, pull some cover over you," Belle said as she rolled over, facing away from him, hoping that would make him more relaxed. When she felt anything but. "I don't bite, honest."

But if you wanted me too, I'd nibble on that bottom lip, then maybe your shoulder, and then— Belle ruthlessly cut that line of thinking. It led nowhere with Mitchell Thomas, and now she'd admit that since Saturday evening when he'd braved the snow to get her key, she'd wished it would.

THE EXTRA WARMTH SLOWLY ROUSED MITCH TO consciousness, and he was ready to push off the blanket until a second later, he registered that a body was pressed up against him.

He shifted a bit, realizing as he moved that an arm was draped across his chest.

Instantly awake, he turned beneath the arm to see Belle's face, mere inches away from his. Her lips slightly apart, each breath sweetly fanning his cheek. Her usually sleek hair was tousled, a few strands resting on her soft porcelain skin.

Heaven help him. Porcelain?

But as he watched her, he realized that indeed was an apt description. She looked fragile and vulnerable at this moment. Yet he'd seen the core of strength that ran through her.

She was facing a difficult decision about her nonprofit. Maybe it wasn't a life-or-death choice, but he'd chosen her nonprofit because the idea, the goal, was important. And for her it was the choice between losing the essence of the concept by turning it over to an über-professional staff that perhaps didn't have the same vision, or perhaps losing her board's support.

He didn't know much about the inner workings of corporate boards, but he did know they wielded a power that was supreme.

Mitch was also guessing that when she started this, her dad and Worth thought it was a good way for her to use her time. Then it became real and tangible: she was able to make a difference, and it was beginning to take a toll on her. But that's what passion did. So why were they so concerned?

He brushed the strands off her cheek, and she stirred slightly.

"What time is it?" she asked, her voice drowsy and sexy.

He cleared his throat. "I have no idea."

"I'm not sure I want to wake up, but my stomach is telling me it needs food."

"It's pretty cozy between us."

Her eyes flew open and a second later, she'd pulled her arm from his chest. Her cheeks bloomed with color, and worry chased the sleep from her eyes.

"Oh, Mitch, that was completely unintended. I'm sorry, I didn't—" She started to scoot away.

"Wait."

She stopped, and he felt her gaze on his.

He tucked that errant strand of hair back into place. Belle leaned into his palm.

As if saying yes.

He leaned forward and captured her mouth beneath his. This time it wasn't going to be a chaste, fast, thank-you kiss. This one he wanted to last.

Wrapping his arm around her, Mitch drew her closer.

Belle sighed softly as she settled against him, then she nibbled at his bottom lip and he groaned.

Breaking their kiss but not moving far from her lips, he canted his leg over hers, then waited, hoping it wasn't too much. She raised her head slightly until their lips met again.

Her eyes turned a dark and smoky green, her lids dipped down. The heat of the kiss turned hotter. The intensity about broke him.

They could make love right now, but what about after? He sensed it would be a disaster to anything that could build between them. He didn't want just sex from Belle Grantham.

He ran a finger down her cheek, then pulled back, reluctantly breaking their kiss.

Her eyes opened wide, and she moved as if to escape his arms, her brow furrowed.

Touching her lips briefly with his, he hoped she understood that he wasn't sorry this happened. How could he be? "It was damn nice to wake up next to you."

Her brow relaxed and a small smile curved her lips. "Ditto, Mitch. Ditto."

PUSHING THE CART THROUGH THE MARKET WITH MITCH beside her felt good, even right. And very domestic. "Mitch, grab an avocado or two will you?"

"The last time I was at the market, all the boys and I were looking for was frozen pizza and brownies," Mitch said. "I don't have a clue about the ripeness of an avocado, sorry. A cantaloupe, yes."

Belle joined him at the pile and picked two. "Cantaloupes are hard. Avocados shouldn't be."

She felt warmth flow through her heart at his burst of laughter.

"I'll teach you about them some day," she promised, then looked to her left.

"Oh, a cheesemonger. This is perfect. A wedge of that Parmesan, please," she asked the woman behind the counter and pointed to the cheese she wanted. Then Belle turned to Mitch, who looked baffled at the numerous cheeses piled upon themselves in the case. "I thought you said you cooked."

"Yes, but fancy cheeses? I'm at a loss."

"Well, wait until you try this with a great sauvignon blanc."

"Okay, got it. A liquor store is the next stop."

Belle wanted to peck his cheek but settled for a smile instead. This really did feel good.

She put a rotisserie chicken and a loaf of crusty olive oil rosemary bread along with some chicken stock into the cart. She found the aisle with the candy and reverently placed two bars of 70% Cacao dark chocolate in with the other items. Last on her list was a bag of French Roast coffee, and she was done.

After a quick stop at the promised liquor store, they were back at her cabin.

"Mitch, will you start the fire?" Belle called from the kitchen as she unpacked the groceries and put the wine in the fridge.

"Already started. I think we'll need more wood since you're staying a couple of extra days. I'll head out to the pile in back and get some. If I don't come back soon, send out the Saint Bernard."

Belle laughed, but remembering Saturday night and the trek he made in the snow, she stopped and rushed to the door. "Wait, maybe you shouldn't do that in the dark—it was treacherous enough Saturday, and now it's had a bit of melt and iced over. How about getting it tomorrow when it's light outside?"

Mitch turned around from putting his boots back on. "Worried about me?"

Belle wondered if he realized just how much his voice had deepened. The huskiness sent shivers all the way to her toes. Her belly was turning to jelly, and she leaned forward. Then caught herself. But it would have been so nice to kiss those lips turned up in a wicked smile.

His blue eyes deepened, and she wondered in a rush of pure feminine curiosity what color they'd turn while making love.

Okay, that did it. Her whole body was jelly now. "You bet. Can't have my number one fan and web guru breaking an arm, now can I?"

The moment was broken, but his smile remained. Thank goodness.

"I'll be fine. I brought a headlamp." He held up a small light attached to an elastic strap. "I can see everything."

Mitch zipped up his jacket, put his headlamp over his hat, and was out the door before she could formulate a coherent reply.

How could she be falling for him?

Shaking her head, she headed back to the kitchen. She

cut up the chicken and put it in a big pan to simmer with the broth and went to work on cubing the bread, putting it on a large platter.

Just as she was arranging the cheese on a wooden plate and pouring the wine, Mitch banged on the door.

She ran to open it, and he came in with his arms full of wood. "Sorry, I can't take off my boots, and I'll track."

"Goodness, I don't care. That's what they make mops for."

He dumped the wood into the wrought iron tub by the fireplace. "Okay, you're set for another couple of fires."

Yeah, like the one you've started in me. So not fair you don't feel it too.

Belle swallowed the words that wanted to come bursting out. "Dinner's simmering, so let's see how you like the cheese."

Mitch took off his boots while Belle brought in the tray with the cheese, the remaining bread, and two glasses of wine. Putting it on the low table in front of the fireplace, she sat staring at the fire until Mitch joined her. She felt a little edgy. This suddenly seemed very intimate after her less-than-innocent thoughts. Yet there was that delicious tingle of realizing the guy next to her was, at least for the moment, all hers.

She cut him a chunk of the fragrant cheese and lifted it toward his mouth. Belle expected him to take it with his fingers. Instead he opened his lips, ready for the bite.

As she placed it gently into his mouth, his lips closed around her fingers. She slowly pulled them out. Talk about an action that went right to the core of her desire. Darn him.

Mitch's eyes twinkled in the firelight's dancing flames, telling her he was well aware of what he was doing.

So maybe, just maybe, he was feeling a bit of the magic between them.

After he'd left to get firewood, she'd turned on two lamps at the back of the living room, so they had firelight in front and a soft glow behind. It would be perfect to be snuggled together on the couch, exploring each other, learning what spots elicited the most intense feelings.

She blinked and returned to the subject of cheese. "What do you think?"

"About? Oh, the cheese?"

Belle looked away quickly and grabbed the wine glasses, handing him one. "Of course, what else?" she said, finally meeting his gaze.

His brow rose as if taunting her. "There are many 'what elses.'" He took a sip of the wine, his gaze not leaving hers. "But back to the cheese—it's really good by itself and even better after a sip of wine. I wonder what else you're going to teach me."

The words by themselves were innocuous, but add in those wicked eyes, and they seemed to be loaded with the promise of fulfillment rather than innocence.

Belle took a sip of the wine and decided, reluctantly, that changing the subject was safer. "I love a roaring fire in winter. Actually anytime. On the ranch, we'd take supplies out to one of the line camps, have a simple dinner, and then drink coffee and watch the stars, all by a campfire.

Usually one of the hands had a guitar or mandolin, and we'd sing or just listen to the music."

Those moments were the only other time Belle had felt at peace with herself since her mama died. And though peace wasn't what she felt around Mitch at the moment, nevertheless it was the same sense of security.

"Someday, I'd like to visit that ranch. I've never been to a working ranch and certainly nothing the size of Trickle Creek. You said your dad brought your mom to the bridge. Just how big is the creek that it needs a bridge?"

Belle laughed and watched Mitch's face mirror his confusion. "In the area of the bridge, it's about 100 feet wide. Not deep there at all. Other places on the ranch, it narrows to about 25 feet with some great fishing spots because it's deep and slow.

"It was named long ago before water was controlled, and it did dry up to a trickle most summers. The bridge is fairly high over that spot, because when it floods it can be a torrent, and then we have to go the long way around to get out."

The timer Belle had set for the simmering chicken went off.

"Dinner's ready. Hungry?"

"Yes."

And she knew it wasn't his stomach he was talking about by his suddenly hooded gaze. He had other appetites on his mind as well.

10

NOTHING WAS SCHEDULED UNTIL THEIR SHOOT AT TWO o'clock. Nevertheless, even though he got home after midnight, he woke at six. The sun wasn't up, his bedroom was dark, and Mitch felt lonely.

He was often alone, but this feeling was directly tied to missing Belle.

Their kiss yesterday was absolutely wrong, and yet absolutely right. Belle was a client. He shouldn't have crossed that professional boundary.

The fact that she wanted that moment to happen as much as he did didn't make him feel better.

The reality that the kiss was filled with wonder and promise and hit him straight in his core was what was right about it.

Even so, he couldn't push away the guilt he always felt when joy or even simple laughter came into his life.

He'd gone to a grief-counseling session after Lauren died. He hadn't wanted to go, but the blackness in his soul needed something. The psychologist labeled it survivor guilt. She told him what he was experiencing was sometimes an unconscious attempt to counteract or undo the helplessness of watching Lauren die.

Of course, knowing all this was the intellectual part of the healing. The emotional part rejected it.

His cell phone buzzed, and he glanced at the number, not intending to answer it. Until he saw it was Belle. "You're supposed to have a lazy morning," he said.

"I know, actually I'm still in bed with a cup of coffee and a square of that chocolate."

God, the image of her tousled, a bit like after their kiss yesterday, went straight to his groin.

"Are you still there?"

Her question brought him back. "Yep. No coffee yet and certainly not a square of chocolate. Though actually right now that sounds good."

He loved her low chuckle. It held the promise of something wonderful. "I was going to go over the layout list and make sure I have the props ready to go. I think the medicine bottle prop is fine. But I'll check it again."

"Mitch, it was perfect when we left your house yesterday. It looked like Greek and that was the perfect image to project for someone who can't read. So make your morning lazy as well...or I have an idea."

Mitch heard the touch of excitement in her voice. "Spill it."

"It's simple really. How about a walk on the Pearl Street Mall. Coffee, maybe breakfast, and then we can head over to the shoot?"

He hesitated. Not because he didn't want to go but because of the kiss. He was the one who initiated it, and he'd been the one to say without words that it was wonderful.

"Mitch, if you're worried about that incredible, mind-blowing kiss we shared, don't be. I won't behave any differently while out in public with you. I won't embarrass you, and we won't repeat it unless you want to."

Again that chuckle and its promise.

"But I can tell you right now. I want to," Belle said.

MITCH TOLD HER HE'D BE BY IN HALF AN HOUR. TRUE TO HIS word, his knock was right on time.

In her haste to get to the airport in Durango, Belle hadn't packed more than a few sweaters, leggings, and jeans. But, from habit, she'd packed plenty of undies, what her Mama called necessities. Something Mama always stressed.

Today Belle was dressed all in black—everything except the undies worn with something else before, but this was the first time she'd worn the outer garments together. Black sweater, black leggings, and her black boots. No hat because the sun was out and the sky more blue than she'd seen in her life.

Brimming with more energy than she'd felt in the last few days since Armie dropped his bombshell, Belle needed to be around people. And especially Mitch.

Thus her idea of strolling the mall.

Watching people would take her mind off her worries, and being with Mitch among the crowds would be fun. It would be interesting to see how he reacted.

There was a solitary vein to Mitch that felt artificial. Not fake, but more like a shell he'd built to protect himself from something. Yet he was a protector. He'd guided her through the airport, shielding her from the chaos of people there. Being on her side with the nonprofit crisis.

Belle opened the door and was pleased to see that Mitch stood there with a smile on his face. She'd been afraid that their kiss had ruined everything. Often it did.

"I'm starved. Where to for breakfast?" she asked as she gathered her small clutch that was both wallet and cell phone carrier.

"How about a Cajun-style breakfast?"

"Like grits and biscuits and eggs?"

"And beignets, which I've never had but want to try," he said.

"You'll love them. I'm on, let's go."

Less than ten minutes later, they'd parked in a lot downtown and were walking west on the mall. Belle stopped at the courthouse on the corner of Fourteenth Street and Pearl. "I remember this building. Now it's all decked out for the holidays. We should come back down at night."

She looked at Mitch and didn't see any reluctance on his face. But then, she couldn't see his eyes, because they both wore sunglasses as the morning sun reflecting off the piles of snow was blindingly bright.

Mitch put an arm around her shoulders and turned

her 180 degrees to face a three-story building on the corner. "The upper floor of that building is Jen's business, ForceOne. She's one of the top digital forensic experts in the world."

There was awe in Mitch's voice when he said that. He fit so well in the cyber world, and yet his creativity and sensitivity to the nuances of a story made what he'd done to her website so extraordinary. "And Brice's office is there as well?"

"Only if one of them didn't want to live."

"What?" Not the couple she saw—they were so much in love.

"I'm kidding, sort of. They've worked on some of Brice's projects together, in fact I have one of them in place on your website, but they have separate offices. Brice's biz wouldn't fit there. He's a cyber-security designer and expert. He has a workforce of a dozen on payroll and more on call who travel over the world installing, troubleshooting, and maintaining his equipment. Jen has two employees and herself, but Brice mentioned she's thinking of adding two more."

Mitch led her down Fourteenth Street, past the Boulder Theater, and Belle stopped to look at the marquee over the sidewalk. "I saw a great concert here that summer I stayed with Maisie. I'm glad to see it's still in business."

"What kind of concert? Rock?"

"Yep. It was a Led Zeppelin tribute band."

"Seriously, you like Zeppelin?"

"It was one of Mama's favs, and I listened to them all the time."

"Goldilocks, *Star Trek*, and Led Zeppelin. What will you surprise me with next?"

He tilted his head and stared at her as if trying to figure it out. Belle simply smirked and raised her brows, taunting him to find out.

She linked her arm through his as they continued down the street.

Mitch stopped on the next block in front of a yellow Victorian house with white gingerbread trim. The sign proclaimed it to be *Lucile's*.

They were seated quickly, ordered chicory coffee, and looked over the vast menu.

Belle put her menu down. "The Cajun breakfast and beignets. Our cook at the ranch grew up in the Mississippi River Delta, and she made the best beignets, won blue ribbons for them. It'll be fun to taste these. You've got to share mine, I can't eat them all."

"Deal."

"Watch out for the powdered sugar."

"And you're wearing all black," he said.

"A napkin or two tucked into my neckline is a necessity with these."

An hour passed as they lingered over after-breakfast coffee, until a line forming for tables made it obvious they needed to leave.

Belle pulled out her wallet only to have Mitch stay her hand. "No, really, it's mine," she protested. "So far you've paid for everything."

"You're on my turf."

"Okay. When you come to Pagosa Springs, I'll return

the favor." Belle looked at him as they walked down the steps of the restaurant and saw the flicker of unease in his eyes before he put on his sunglasses. "What?"

"Nothing."

"Mitch, whatever you're going to say isn't going to ruin my day. Promise. Besides, you usually speak your mind about everything."

That got a small grin out of him.

"Do you think you'll stay there? It sounded like Worth really wanted you to move to a larger city. Boulder *is* close to Denver."

Ohhh, does he want me close by?

Her heart did a little trip-hammer dance, then she mentally sighed, realizing too late that the sound left her lips.

"Uh, oh. That doesn't sound good."

"I told Armie when he called that I needed another year. We'll have your website, and I'm going to focus on finding celebrities, including Armie, to support the cause. I *didn't* tell him that if it's still not where we..." Belle stressed *we*, meaning her board and herself... *And wouldn't it be nice if Mitch were part of the we.*

As what? A boyfriend? A consultant?

It sounded like he might want to be...one of those.

"Where we want it to be," she continued, "I'll give in if the deal is still on the table by then. I know I need a couple of staffers, and I think I'll look for some volunteers or at least part-time paid workers."

Mitch pulled her into a hug. "I think that's a great compromise. Though I'd like to have you a bit closer."

Belle loved being hugged in the middle of the day, in the middle of a sidewalk, not caring who saw it. It felt wonderful and like being a part of a couple she'd mused about just seconds ago. She tightened her arms around him, and they stood for a moment locked in the hug.

Then Mitch stepped back. But he didn't break their contact; this time he linked arms with her.

"Now, let's wander this amazing street, and you can help me buy a couple of Christmas presents for Papa and Junior before we head off to the shoot."

IT HAD BEEN EYE-OPENING TO WATCH BELLE SHOP. NOT ONCE did she look at a price tag. If the cashmere men's scarf would look good on her dad, she bought it. If the running jacket would work for her brother, she bought it.

She put a huge amount of thought into every gift. It wasn't throwing money at a gift or being lavish, it was the right gift. Not that he knew her father or her brother, but it was the way she looked at, then thought through the selection as she talked to herself.

And that green silk sweater she modeled for him before she bought it? She did look phenomenal in it. And after he said so, Belle, with a grin, just handed over her credit card and wore it out of the store. He'd seen the price, and it wasn't cheap.

"I want to get Maisie something for letting me use the cabin, but I don't see just the right thing yet," Belle said as they passed Broadway and headed west. "Maybe some earrings. She loves earrings."

"I heard Annie mentioning that a guy named Todd Reid made some great jewelry set with raw diamonds."

"Ohhh, I want to see those before I leave. They might be perfect for her."

Belle's comment highlighted the difference between the normal consumer and the rich ones.

Granted he could buy any of the items she'd purchased. But he'd ponder the price, mentally tally up everything, then decide.

It was habit, no longer necessity.

Belle was the exact opposite. Her habit was to look for the right gift and damn the cost. Being honest with himself, he knew he'd never change. Nor would she. And then he realized it was okay. Belle wasn't haughty or superior. In fact she'd laughed and listened to the sales woman when she offered advice on a gift.

Belle didn't act rich or privileged.

And the moment that thought dawned on him, he recalled one of his professors at Radford telling his students he was retiring. His parting words were, "This is my advice to you all. You're smart, you'll all make a lot of money, but remember there is only one thing money buys you and that is the freedom to do what you want."

Instantly, in the middle of Pearl Street Mall, his perceptions crumbled into dust. She was using her money to do what she wanted and that was the nonprofit. Nobody had the right to take that away.

He'd fight to the proverbial death to keep that from happening.

Mitch took her arm and wished he could tell her, but that would simply be over the top. They walked back down the mall, watching buskers pantomiming and creating magic tricks. Belle pulled him to a stop in front of a choral group in old English costumes singing carols.

"I love Christmas, don't you?" she asked as the group paused between songs.

Mitch was saved from answering when a little boy chasing his sister ran right into his legs. He fell backwards on his rump and started to wail.

Belle bent down to see if he was hurt just as his frantic mother rushed up to him.

"You're okay, sweetie." She picked him up. "He's fine, just more startled than hurt. I'm sorry he ran into you," she said, cuddling her son.

"No worries," Mitch said, making sure the boy heard it too.

The mom grasped both children's hands and kept them close to her as they left the crowd.

"Merry Christmas," Belle called.

Mitch felt a jab in his ribs. "Merry Christmas," he echoed, realizing that with his nephews out of town, he'd almost forgotten that Christmas was so close. Even though they'd just been shopping for presents, it wasn't on his radar.

This year, he'd have no one to share it with. Even though he and Cole didn't exchange gifts, they both bought the boys a stack of presents. They were young enough to still enjoy ripping into them. Even Belle would be with her family back in Pagosa Springs.

He'd be alone.

The chirping of his phone alarm finally penetrated his consciousness. Pulling out the insistent machine, he glanced at the time. "We gotta pick up the props and head to the shoot. Ready?"

"Yep, excited. Promise me though, we can come back here at night when the lights are all on."

"Cross my heart."

Her laughter chased away his momentary feeling of loneliness. It would be lovely to walk the mall with her, hand in hand. Maybe steal a kiss or two ... or three.

IT TOOK LONGER THAN THE TEN MINUTES IT HAD THIS morning to navigate the traffic back to his house. He left the SUV running in the driveway with Belle inside and ran in to his office to gather his box of props.

Belle found a Pandora station of Christmas music on the car's stereo.

"So where is this studio?" she asked, pausing her humming to the music.

"The studio is in No-Bo, or North Boulder," he said, after finally making it through the last crazy stop light, and headed up the hill on Broadway. "It's the hip, newish area of Boulder, lots of lofts and condos."

"Isn't this the way to Jennifer and Brice's house?"

"Good memory."

As if on cue, the phone connection in the car rang. Mitch pushed the talk button on the steering wheel. "Jennifer, serendipitous that you called. We're on Broadway and just passed your street. What's up?"

"The tree trimming party is tonight, and since you said 'we're,' I'm assuming Belle is still in town. Can you both come?"

From the corner of his eye, Mitch saw Belle nod vigorously. Well, why not? He liked Jen and Brice, and as Belle said, nobody was missing her back in Pagosa Springs. Then he wondered how that was possible. Belle was too full of life not to have a million friends. "Thanks, we'd both enjoy it. What time?"

Jen's five thirty answer gave them plenty of time at the studio as he'd only booked three hours.

Mitch pulled into the parking lot of a somewhat dilapidated building.

"This is it? It doesn't look hip or new."

"Don't let the outside fool you," Mitch cautioned. "The look is on purpose. Notice there's no sign on the building. Again on purpose."

They buzzed in on an intercom, and the door lock released for them. They followed the old and tattered green carpet and made a right turn. There the interior changed with bright lighting and new, soft wool carpeting. He smiled as Belle's mouth dropped open. "It's just in case people get nosey and try to look inside.

"All this for a photography studio? It's amazing."

"This is a co-op building. It houses a trio of photographers and their shared studio space as well as a couple of start-up software companies and the headquarters for Super Gizmo.

"Oh. I love their games. I play Warrior Princess on my iPad."

"Okay, Goldilocks, Trekkie, Zeppelin lover, and now gamer?"

"Just a couple of games. I play the princess game, a farm game, and that insidious candy game."

They entered the studio with its rolls of seamless paper, photo lights, various chairs, and tables stacked against a back wall.

Minka, the photographer, who wore his silver hair long and tied in a black ribbon at the back of his head, introduced them to his half-dozen models, including the young son and daughter of one. The kids were in a couple of the scenes Mitch had planned.

Mitch's intense work paid off, and with Minka's help, the shots were set up quickly. Then Mitch and Belle stood back and allowed the magic of the photographer and models to work the feeling of the scene.

Set up after set up, Minka took hundreds of images. Then came time for the final set up.

This was the image that Mitch knew Belle wanted to be perfect.

When Minka started shooting, Belle moved closer to Mitch, then after a few minutes she put her arm around his waist and leaned her head on his shoulder. "It's all pretty real, isn't it?" she whispered. "That look of terror on her face, the boy looking so sick. Poor Mama, I can't imagine what she went through."

Mitch heard her stifled sob, wrapped his arm around her, and pulled Belle closer. The studio wasn't dark, and they certainly weren't alone, but it felt like it to him. Like they were in an oasis apart from, but viewing, a reality.

Even for him, who dealt with images and words on one side and the practical technical work on the other side of his business, this moment with Belle, seeing the sense of how hard life was for those who couldn't read, played havoc with his heart.

"Belle, believe me when I say I'll do whatever I can to help you keep and grow Goal 100%."

The shine of tears lingered in her green eyes as she looked up at him. "I believe you will," she said softly. "You understand."

Belle leaned against him again, and he kissed the top of her shining cap of hair.

He heard her sigh.

Then the shoot was done.

Belle lingered with one of the models, and when she turned around, he whistled. The smoky look the model had created on Belle made the green of her eyes stand out.

She was stunning.

It was time to head to Jen and Brice's. Mitch was actually looking forward to this party. And knew it was because Belle would be there with him.

He might pay for it tonight when he was alone and the guilt over Lauren flooded him. But for now he was determined to make the moment last.

11

As Mitch pulled into the cobbled driveway in front of Jennifer and Brice's house, Belle glanced in the visor mirror one more time. She'd asked one of the models to teach her how to put on that smoky-eyed look that was the rage. She watched in the mirror as the model did her right eye and then helped Belle do the left. The woman fixed the areas where Belle messed up.

When Belle turned around to face Mitch, he'd whistled. So she figured it looked as good as she thought it did.

Since her new look had been received so well and she'd decided on the course she was going to take with her board, she felt energized and positive that she could make it work. So she was really looking forward to the party. Almost as an exclamation point to her day.

The fact that Mitch had offered his continued support and had said the magic words "believe me" made her almost giddy with relief.

Armie's suggestion had punctured her belief in everybody. If her best and oldest friend and her papa could turn on her, who could she believe in?

Mitch.

He escorted her inside and, having been there only a couple of days ago, she instinctively headed for the kitchen area to see if there was anything she could do to help. Jennifer was there along with another woman and two men. The woman was dressed all in black and the man beside her was her mate, if the arm around her was any indication. The second man kept rearranging the platter of yummy looking appetizers. Belle wanted to pluck one right off the plate but somehow got the impression the man wouldn't like it.

Jennifer wiped her hands on a towel and came right to Belle, kissing her on the cheek. "We're so glad you and Mitch could come. Please meet Todd Sargent, Susan Hancock, and her fiancé, Kirk. Mitch, I think you met Todd and Susan at the office."

Susan and Kirk greeted them like old friends. Todd cocked his head to the side, then finally handed her the toast with tomatoes and goat cheese that was in the exact center of his platter.

Then, before she could thank him, he lifted the platter and carried it into the living room.

"Todd likes you. He's an absolute genius. Odd, but smart," Susan said softly with a wink at Jennifer, who simply smiled.

Within half an hour the house was full of people. Mitch didn't leave her side, unless it was to get her another glass of wine, so they met everyone as a couple. Occasionally, since he was so tall, he was pulled away to hang an ornament near the top of the tree.

"Hey, Mitch, Belle, come in here, Annie's on Facetime," Jennifer called from the kitchen.

"Merry Christmas, Mitch, and nice to meet you, Belle." Annie laughed and Belle liked her instantly. Just as she liked her hosts. Mitch had great people surrounding him. She had the sense he didn't realize it.

"Annie, your Christmas lights are simply amazing. I can't wait to see it all again. Mitch will have to drive me past the house again tonight."

"How long are you going to be in Boulder? Jen is going to do my usual cider duty on Christmas eve, so if you're around, stop by."

"Hey, can we talk to Uncle Mitch?" Two boys' voices sounded off screen, interrupting them.

And in a flash, Annie had disappeared to be replaced by two heads jostling for screen time. "Uncle Mitch, guess what? We got to go SNUBA at Huna..hana." The adorable younger boy wrinkled his brow over the name.

"Hanauma Bay," said the older of them. "And tomorrow we're going to ride an outrigger."

"Hey, Josh and Pete, that sounds like fun. I miss you guys. Say hi to Belle."

Both faces looked at her expectantly. "Hi, guys. Your Uncle Mitch tells me you love to snowshoe. It's cold here—wanna trade places?"

Josh, the younger one, giggled in that cute, little-boy way.

"Nah, we're good here," Pete said.

"Yeah, that's what I thought you'd say. Well, we'll keep some snow for you so you'll have some when you get back."

Mitch and the boys chatted another couple of minutes. As Belle watched Mitch's face, she saw his love for the boys shine through. He really did adore his nephews. She wondered what Lauren had looked like. If she had only part of Mitch's smile and eyes, she'd have been a knockout.

Then another man came on. "Hi, Belle, I'm Cole, these guys' poor beleaguered father."

"Dad" was the choral whine behind him.

"I hope I get to meet you in person when we get home. Mitch, everything okay with the house?"

"Perfect. Lots of snow and Brice is keeping the walks plowed. So enjoy the sun and fun."

A startled look filled Cole's eyes, then he beamed a smile. "Mele Kalikimaka. Merry Christmas."

"Merry Christmas" came from their own chorus of Mitch, Jennifer, Brice, and her.

The screen went blank.

"That was fun. Nice people, and the boys are adorable."

Brice slipped away and started playing carols on the grand piano in the living room that Jen had mentioned he'd moved here from his house in the DC area. He played like a pro. Belle grabbed Mitch's hand and headed in that direction, with Jennifer bringing up the rear.

They sang for a good thirty minutes when Belle noticed that Jennifer was moving into the kitchen and turned to follow her. Mitch started to come with her.

"I'm just going to help her—I'll be back in a second," she said.

Belle felt his gaze on her the entire distance to the kitchen, and when she turned around, she caught him staring at her.

"I saw that. You and Mitch seem to have some chemistry happening."

Belle felt heat flooding her face. "He's a great guy, funny, talented, smart."

Jen's look was nearly disbelieving. "Well, something you've done has turned him around."

"Around? From what, a grinch?"

"Pretty much. It took Annie months to get him to smile when she was around. He very much resented her taking Lauren's place."

"But Lauren died. Mitch adores his nephews. He wouldn't have wanted them not to have a mom around to love and cherish them."

Jen simply shrugged. "I like Mitch, now. But until a month before the wedding, it was touch and go. I think the boys moved him from frozen to lukewarm. And until now, it seemed he didn't want to be around us, though we'd invited him. So as I said, you've worked some magic on him. And I'm glad." Jennifer grasped a tray. "Grab the other one if you don't mind."

"Happy to, and thanks for inviting us. I haven't had much Christmas yet, so this was really nice."

"Mitch isn't the only one who likes you. Brice and I consider you a friend, a good friend."

Warmth flooded Belle, and she wondered if that's how Mitch thought about her. It'd be a good start.

To what?

To something more than friends.

Jennifer passed around the platter of filled eggnog cups. Belle put pretty Christmas-y plates of rum balls, cookies, and spice cake on the coffee table and the dining room table.

"To Christmas and good friends here to help celebrate the season," Brice toasted and raised his cup.

Everyone followed suit and drank when he did.

"Okay. Everybody ready?"

At the chorus of yeses, Brice turned off all the lights and instantly the tree bloomed with lights in all the colors of Christmas. The ornaments they'd put on sparkled merrily.

It was glorious.

"It's so beautiful," Belle whispered under her breath.

Mitch pulled her closer, and she wrapped her arm around him and squeezed.

For an instant she thought it was too bad that she had to go back to Pagosa Springs in time to be there for Papa and Junior. Then she felt instantly ashamed, putting her happiness before theirs. Maybe Mitch would come back with her. Dare she ask?

A few moments later, the lights came back on, except for the area over the tree. It still sparkled in the dusky shadows.

"How did you guys work that magic?" Belle asked loudly enough for Brice to hear.

"It was Todd. He rerouted some circuits and it's all on remote control.

"I love it. Great job, Todd."

The man blushed and looked a bit uncomfortable to be the sudden center of attention.

"We've gotta go. Kirk is on call from midnight to midnight, and I've got a tough case to work on bright and early," Susan said as she took the platter of empty cups into the kitchen.

People started to leave and many stopped under the mistletoe to smooch. Belle wondered if she and Mitch would.

Jennifer got their coats and as they walked under the mistletoe, Mitch pulled her into a dip and kissed her soundly. It ended all too quickly but earned applause from the rest of the guests.

Belle blushed and Mitch grinned as he escorted her out the door into the cold night. As warm as she was on the inside, she didn't even bother zipping up her parka.

"Do you want to come in for a glass of wine?" Belle asked at the front door of the cabin.

Yes, and maybe more, but none of that is wise. I've laughed and felt happier today than in a long, long time. "Are you tired? We've had nothing but late nights," he said instead of any of the things he'd been thinking.

"No, surprisingly I'm not. But, Mitch, it's okay if you've

had enough of me for the day. We've spent a lot of time together. Don't feel guilty about saying no."

"Belle, it's not that."

"Then can you tell me what's the matter? Did I say something at the party I shouldn't have?"

Mitch leaned against the door jam and crossed his arms. He shook his head slowly. "No, people loved being around you—who wouldn't? It was that kiss. It was ... incredible."

"Oh, is that all? That's not a problem, at least for me. Come in and get out of the cold and tell me why you think for a minute it could be an issue."

Her laugh was gentle and inviting, and unexpectedly he wanted to tell Belle everything.

Mitch started a fire while Belle was in the kitchen, getting the wine.

She came out bearing two glasses and the last of the Parmesan cheese on two plates.

Mitch sat at one end of the leather couch, and Belle sat at the other. It was a four-person couch, so there was room between them. He didn't want the room, but he did want to watch her face as he told her his story.

Not sure where to start, he stared at the fire, watching the embers flare up the chimney, listening to the wood crackle and pop.

"At the beginning is always good," she said softly.

He smiled in spite of himself and turned to face her. "Lauren was younger by only two years, but at first that was an eon of difference for me. My parents had no idea how to parent. However, they had a knack for losing money. They tried every get-rich scheme they could find. In between those failures, they would work hard to make enough for the next golden egg to hatch. So I started taking care of my sister at a very young age. No one at home to potty-train her, so she was in diapers too long. I trained her and I was four, not much out of diapers myself. I cooked for her, meaning we ate a lot of cereal. I helped her learn to spell, and ..."

He stopped and raked a hand through his hair. "You get the picture. When she was old enough, she learned to really cook beside me. It was only in high school, where I met Cole, that we'd actually have a place to go and feel cared for. His parents' house was our refuge. I know my own parents didn't realize we spent more time there than at our house."

He took a long sip of wine and sputtered as it went down too fast. Compassion warred with anger on Belle's face. Yet she said nothing to interrupt him. And he appreciated that—he was on a roll. Other than Cole, no one knew these things.

"I worked at a restaurant and moved up the ladder to bartender so I could be home to make sure Lauren had dinner and did her homework, then I left for work. Cole and I went to different colleges. I got a scholarship, thank God. Lauren went to George Mason, Cole's school, and fairly soon they moved from sister-of-my-buddy to a couple. Before that"—Mitch laughed at the memory—"Lauren would tail us, always showing up at awkward times, like on date night at a movie or at chess club or ice hockey training."

Belle smiled. "I can absolutely see that."

"After they got married, I got the job in Denver at Web Wizards and moved West. I still saw them as much as I could. They had the boys, Cole got his PhD, and life was pretty good for all of us. Then Lauren got sick. She refused to move to a state where transplants were easier to get, and I only found out recently that she refused Cole as a donor, because if the cancer were genetic, one of the boys might need Cole's kidney." Mitch couldn't look at Belle, worried that she'd think he was a jerk, but he needed to get it all out. "I wasn't very nice to Cole for a long time, thinking he was a cop-out, a chicken."

Belle scooted across the couch, and sat cross-legged beside him, her knees touching him. It felt good to have the physical connection, even as minor as it was.

"I was a match, but we had to wait for a process called plasmapheresis to remove the antibodies out of her blood that would have caused rejection. She had cascading organ failure before she was clean."

Firelight reflected on the wet tear streaks on Belle's cheeks. He wanted to brush them away, but needed to finish his story.

Needed to explain. Not to just anyone, only to Belle.

"I couldn't save her. All my life until she and Cole fell in love, I took care of her. And at the end there was nothing I could do. Cole and I sat in that hospital room practically twenty-fours a day. Praying for a miracle. Anything. The boys were staying with friends but wanted to see their mom, so we told them to come whenever they wanted to. Going to school that last week of Lauren's life wasn't an issue. Cole and I were there when she took her last soft breath.

"She was gone. And I felt so guilty. And every time I have fun or feel light-hearted, I feel guilty that I'm still here. I'm alive. I couldn't save her."

Belle took the wineglass from his fingers and put it on the table with her own. Then she wrapped her arms around his neck and touched her forehead to his. It was the most comforting gesture she could have made.

"It takes time to heal. Lauren for you, just like Mama for me, will never leave you. But believe me when I say I've learned you can't feel guilty for living. The greatest gift you can give the boys is to recall their mother with love, not guilt. Not anger, not sadness, but with happiness and joy and love.

"And guilt destroys that," Belle whispered.

Mitch felt the wetness of his own tears on his cheeks but did nothing to wipe them away.

Belle put just enough distance between them to reach up and thumb the tears away for him.

"I had practically the exact opposite of your life, and Mama died suddenly, not from an illness. But the pain is no different. My legacy for her is Goal 100%, and for you, until you find a mate and perhaps have children, your legacy is those adorable boys."

Belle got up and crooked her finger to him to do the same.

He had no idea what was going on in her head.

But instead of heading to the bedroom, she walked to the front door. "I'm kicking you out for your own good. We both need each other tonight. But if and when this happens, I want it between us with no guilt, no ghosts —just us."

She handed him his parka and hat. "Go home, let yourself heal. You're a great uncle, a talented web designer, and a helluva dipper."

That made Mitch smile just before he wrapped her in his arms and took her lips in a short but powerful kiss. "Now, can you add great kisser to that list?"

"It was already on it."

12

MITCH WOKE BEFORE DAWN AND LAY STILL BETWEEN THE soft, warm sheets. He took stock of his body: no tension running up his back, no tight jaw.

His eyes burned a bit, but after the tears last night he expected that. Then it hit him. A tingle of anticipation, of wanting to jump out of bed. Not because he had to but because he was going to see Belle soon.

He waited, his eyes roaming the dark bedroom, and waited some more. The guilt that he was still breathing wasn't there. As soon as he thought it, a bit of the pain and prick of that old emotion surfaced, but it didn't overpower his joy or cloud his judgment.

Glancing at the clock, he realized 6 a.m. was too early to implement the idea that had come to him last night when they were face-timing with Annie. Hawaii time was what, three hours or so earlier?

Instead he composed text messages to Annie and Jen

and hoped they both had their phones on do-not-disturb until they woke up.

Dressing quickly, and heading downstairs to his office, he worked at his computer until his phone alarm went off. Twelve o'clock already? Time to pick up Belle, grab a sandwich, and head to the studio to look at the proofs.

As he neared her cottage, a moment of unease hit him. Until he realized they'd shared something rare: confidences with no judgment. And they'd parted the best possible way, with a kiss and humor.

Nothing to be uneasy about.

And amazingly, the uneasiness left him.

Before he parked the car, Belle was out the door. "I can't wait, let's go."

"We have time for lunch and I'm starving. I didn't eat this morning."

"Why?" She put a hand to her mouth. "Oh, no, I can't believe we haven't gone to the market for you. Just for our dinner at the cabin. You poor starving man."

"It wasn't just the lack of food, though there is peanut butter and crackers in the fridge—I was busy."

"Doing what?"

"I'll tell you later, maybe," he said, giving her a wink.

"Not fair at all," Belle said, with a pretend pout, and crossed her arms.

She wolfed down her sandwich at Breadworks and was tapping her fingers on the table while he finished his. He just ate slower … taking maybe six bites to her three.

Her wrinkled nose told him she knew exactly what he was doing.

Two hours later they were back at the cabin, and Belle was unlocking the wooden door. "I still can't believe how Minka got the tone just right. It was all your preplanning that made it work. Total genius at work."

Mitch followed her inside, smiling at the almost nonstop excitement Belle vibrated with since they saw the proofs at Minka's studio.

"And I can't believe he got them done so quickly."

"Digital images, Belle. He's going to clean them up a bit and send them to me over the Internet. I'll change the backgrounds to match the narrative, turn the major shot sequences into a mini video that will play automatically on the site when that specific page is opened, and we'll be done."

"Done? You mean as in the site will be up and running?"

"Yup. Once you approve, I'll activate this new one and take down your old one. It's seamless."

"I can't wait. That will show Papa and Armie that I mean business. We'll have to get a bottle of champagne to celebrate. I couldn't have done any of this without you and your incredible talent."

The next second Belle wrapped him in a bear hug and pulled his head so her lips could meet his.

It's a simple thank-you kiss. Don't read more into it, Mitch, old man.

A sharp rap on the front door surprised them both.

"Belladonna?" Armstrong Worth's voice boomed through the door.

Mitch looked at Belle, stunned. "Worth?"

"Armie?" she said simultaneously.

Alarm suddenly filled Belle's face, and Mitch remembered her mother had been taken from them suddenly. He knew she was thinking about her family and a potential crisis if Armie was here. She ran the short distance to the door and flung it open.

Crowding the front door were Worth and two other men. He suspected one was Dutch Grantham and the other Junior.

"Papa! Junior!"

Mitch heard the unmistakable relief in her voice. This wasn't about them.

Dutch Grantham was as tall or maybe a skosh taller than he was and had close-cropped gray hair threaded with the same auburn as Belle's. Junior stood an inch or so shorter and had sandy brown hair. Both men looked very uncomfortable but gave Belle real, loving smiles. At any other time, Mitch thought he'd like them.

Right now he was pretty sure they weren't here just to celebrate the holiday.

"What are you all doing here? I thought you were coming to Pagosa Springs on the twenty-fourth."

Mitch watched as her relief turned to suspicion.

"It's only two days early, Princess. I'm so happy to see you."

Belle's face reflected her warring emotions. Mitch knew she loved her papa and brother and that Armie was her close buddy. But seeing them all together at her front door and apparently unexpected, Mitch knew as she did that this didn't bode well for her.

His blood pounded through his veins; his fight instinct was kicking in. He had to be polite, but that facade wouldn't last long if someone he cared about was in danger of being hurt. Physically or having their dream squashed.

Cared about?

His mind paused for a second, and then he acknowledged the emotion his heart knew and what his mind took longer to accept. He more than cared about Belle, he loved her.

How was this possible in such a short time?

It was love at first sight—Cole is the man for me. Lauren's words played in his head. He had his answer.

"Can we come in?" Dutch Grantham asked.

BELLE BACKED AWAY FROM THE DOOR. SHE MOTIONED THE three people she loved—but didn't want to see at this moment—into the cabin. "Of course."

As Armie passed her, she gave him a look that would have scorched most humans. He deflected it easily as he always did when trouble was brewing by flashing her his "only for Belle" smile.

This time it didn't work and he cocked his head, a questioning look in his eye.

Belle ignored it.

After she firmly closed the door behind them, she looked at Mitch. He moved to stand beside her, and she had her answer. He was staying and he was on her side. Or at least the nonprofit's side. Which in her mind were one and the same.

They followed the trio into the living room and fully expected them to sit wherever they pleased. After all they were still her family. But they stood, and she hated the tension in the air. "Please, make yourselves at home. I have wine and coffee."

Papa looked at her. "I think coffee would be welcomed by everyone."

"Dutch Grantham," he introduced himself to Mitch, sticking out his hand for a quick shake. "You've met Armstrong, and that fellow next to him is my son, Junior."

"Sir," Mitch said.

Belle turned for the kitchen and saw from the corner of her eye that Mitch followed her in. They said nothing as she filled the tank with water and the basket with her French Roast. Ever the hostess, she put cream and sugar, napkins and spoons on a tray.

Then waited as the coffee finished brewing.

Mitch touched her shoulder and when she turned from the counter, held open his arms. She stepped into them. And felt safer than she had in months, ever since it had become apparent that Goal 100% wasn't meeting the expectations of her board.

She couldn't stop her shivers, but being in the safety of his arms helped warm her.

"I'm here, we can fight this," he whispered into her hair. "I'm here."

And she knew he was. He'd not leave her to fight this alone. And fight she would.

BELLE'S HANDS SHOOK SO MUCH THAT MITCH TOOK THE TRAY from her and followed her out to the living room.

He admired the way she held her head high, but he was the one who handed the cups around as she tucked her hands into her jeans pockets to hide their tremble.

Mitch wished there was a fire in the fireplace, but now was not the time to build an actual fire. Especially since it was already simmering inside Belle. It was time to get out in the open whatever the trio came for.

She waited until her guests had taken their first sip. "So, Papa, can I guess what brings *my* board to me at this particular time?"

"No need to guess. Armie was worried enough about the nonprofit *and* you that as soon as he returned from England, he chartered a jet and here we are."

"I told him I needed more time."

"Belle, I know you well enough that when you say something like that, it pretty much always means no," Worth said with a touch of sadness in his voice. "I even thought about leaving the board, but—"

"Princess, we're both businessmen and see the potential of the nonprofit with the right team. Besides, Belle, you've been working yourself to death over this. Yes, it's a great concept, but you can't do all the work. It's impossible," Papa said.

"This is my baby. I'm doing it for Mama, to honor her and her method, to make sure that no one has to go through what she did. Women who need to read need me."

"They need literacy, Belle."

Mitch watched as she literally buckled, then stood straight. Belle gasped and gasped again.

He moved closer, ready to catch her if she fainted.

Worth rose from the couch to do the same. She waved him away.

"You said this before, Armie, that there would be a talented staff, that it would be run professionally. So what you don't need is me."

13

"Princess, you know that isn't true—"

"Isn't it, Papa? You were proud of me when I started this, believing it to be the best testament to Mama's strength and the methods she developed. It still is. That hasn't changed."

Junior got up and approached her. Mitch moved closer. Even though he was the brother she loved, and the man who was standing up for her was a stranger in many ways, she felt closer to Mitch than her family at this moment.

"Junior, please sit down." She waited until he'd returned to his chair. "Now what did you want to say?"

"Sis, it's simply that we've noticed you're exhausted and have been for a year or more. As Dad said, this is taking a toll on you."

"It's a toll I'm willing to bear, as you are with the goats and the brand you're trying to build, Trickle Creek Gourmet Goat Cheese." She answered her brother, then looked directly at Armie. "Didn't you work insane hours trying to get Worth Investments established?"

"I did, and when I got to a point where I could hire the staff to make me better, I did exactly that. Belle, I hired the best I could find, and I do my best to keep them."

"But you started with seed money and you had to make it work. It took a toll on you, but you recovered."

She turned toward Papa. "And you," she pointed at him. "You've told me stories about your father starting the ranch and how you added to it when you could, buying more and more land and cattle. Working right alongside the hands when you couldn't afford more help. You built Trickle Creek Ranch into what it is today. It was hard, but you survived, and that's what I'm doing. Papa, I'm asking as your daughter, don't do this to me, to Mama's legacy."

"Princess, what you don't know and I've never told you, is that exhaustion and overwork is what killed your mama. She fell asleep at the wheel, exhausted after the charity auction that followed a fund-raising dinner, following her address to the state legislature over literacy funding. She ran a red light and was T-boned. I can't, I will not have that same thing happen to you."

Stunned, Belle didn't know what to do or say and stood rooted, mouth open in shock.

Papa rose slightly from his place on the leather couch, then his eyes grew round and he clutched his chest, falling sideways onto Armie.

Belle heard a scream and only seconds later realized it was hers.

DUTCH GRANTHAM WAS NOW FIGHTING FOR HIS LIFE UNDER the care of an army of nurses in intensive care, following a triple bypass. It had been a long surgery and the tension in the waiting room was sickeningly heavy.

Sometime soon, Belle, along with Junior, would be allowed into that ICU room, helping Dutch in his fight. He wouldn't know they were there, but hopefully he'd feel the strength of their love.

Mitch hated being here with every fiber of his body. Naturally, it brought back memories of Lauren's last days.

Then as now there was absolutely nothing to be done; he was powerless. He'd never been the kind of person to stand by and watch, wait. If something needed fixing or taking care of, Mitch did it, sometimes not asking permission, just solving the problem.

While it wasn't his loved one in critical care, the woman he loved was going through the same hell. Had twice, once with her mom and now with her dad.

Mitch went to the coffee machine and brought Belle another cup of hot brew and took her half-drunk coffee away. "Here, try this."

Her wan smile twisted his heart. "I think I'm coffee'd out, but thank you."

"It's chamomile tea. It'll help you relax, or so I've heard." He sat on the couch next to her, wishing he could eradicate her pain along with the guilt he knew was mixed in, that Dutch's heart attack was her fault. Totally false.

Nevertheless, Belle was caught tightly in guilt's insidious grip.

Armie came over and kissed the top of her head. "Now that Dutch is out of surgery, I'm heading to the cafeteria to make a business call, then I'll grab a bite. Are you sure you don't want anything?"

She shook her head.

Armie looked at him.

"Maybe we'll wander down after Dutch is awake," Mitch said.

Belle moved from the couch to kneel by Junior's chair. "Go with Armie. We'll be fine and I'll call you the minute Papa wakes up."

"I don't think I should leave you or Dad."

"I've got Mitch. Go on, I'll call you the moment Papa is awake."

I've got Mitch. As tense as the moment was, Mitch felt those three words all the way to his heart.

Her words gave him hope that maybe there was something more between them than her nonprofit and his website.

Although there were a few other people in the room, it was big enough to give them privacy in their seating group.

He watched Belle and Junior together and thought of his sister and how much they'd loved each other. They brought Cole and eventually the boys into their circle. What a fool he'd been to push any of them away. Or try to bribe them for their continued love. He needed to tell them and Annie as soon as possible that they were the most precious gift of all.

Mitch looked out the expanse of windows in the ICU waiting room to the view beyond. Night had fallen, the sky was clear.

As were his head and heart. He felt better than he had in years.

After Armie and Junior left the room, Belle came back and sat next to him on the couch. Thigh touching thigh. Shoulder touching shoulder. She held out her hand palm up.

When Mitch clasped it and held it tight, Belle lowered her head to his shoulder. He brought their hands to his lips and kissed her fingers. "Just keep remembering, the doc said the surgery was successful. Now it's time for him to heal, and you'll have your papa back. Hale and hearty."

MITCH DIDN'T KNOW HOW LONG THEY WAITED AS HE TRIED to give his Belle strength. Finally a nurse entered the waiting room and made a beeline to them. "Your father is awake now. Don't be worried that he still has a breathing tube inserted. It'll be there for a while yet."

Belle jumped up, and Mitch expected her to head immediately down the corridor. Instead she hugged him hard, then pulled his head down until her lips met his. "Thank you for believing. Come with me, please." As they headed down the corridor past the sliding glass walls of each room, she dialed her phone.

"He's awake," she said to her brother.

Mitch stayed just inside the broad glass door, watching

Belle and Dutch reunite. Tears streamed down her face, and Dutch just barely had the strength to brush them away. Speech was impossible for him because of the tube down his throat.

Junior burst into the room with Armie bringing up the rear. Worth stayed near the door beside Mitch. Dutch Grantham was surrounded by his kids and their love.

Mitch didn't even know if his parents were still alive. But seeing this kind of familial love was reinforcement to what he had now. What he had to grasp, yet hold gently.

Just then his phone vibrated, and he looked at the screen. Annie got his text and was calling back. "I'll be back in a minute if Belle wonders where I've gone. I need to take this," he whispered to Armie.

He headed back to the North West waiting room and out to its balcony. It was cold but refreshing. "Hey, Annie, sorry, I'm in the ICU of the hospital. Belle's dad had a triple bypass."

"I thought he lived in Texas."

"Long story, but his visit had to do with that deadline I told you about. Did you get any good news?"

"Oh yeah, just wait until you hear the number of authors and big wigs that Jen and I have worked."

Mitch smiled for the first time in hours. He might not be able to fix the trauma that Belle was now going through, but his idea was definitely something he and his friends could make happen. "Annie, if you weren't so far away, I'd kiss you. Thank you for making this work. I'll call Jen in a bit and thank her. I can't wait to tell Belle."

"Mitch?"

"Yes?"

"I think your heart has grown three sizes bigger."

He chuckled. "I think you're right."

14

THE LAST DAY AND A HALF PASSED IN A BLUR OF FEAR AND relief. Belle knew that Papa had a long road of rehab in front of him. And as stubborn as he was, he'd take it on with a vengeance so he could be back to one hundred percent or better.

When she'd passed the nurses station on one of her many trips to and from Papa's room, Belle glanced at the calendar and realized today was Christmas Eve. She was supposed to be picking up Papa and Junior from the Durango airport. Not resting on a recliner, watching a heart monitor. She glanced at her brother, also in Papa's room, catching a nap on the pull-out couch. It all felt very surreal.

Earlier in the day Papa's breathing tube had been removed, and though he could talk, his voice was raspy.

As if by mutual consent, nobody talked about the nonprofit. But before the day was done, she'd announce the decision she'd come to.

She wasn't happy about it, but that wasn't the issue. Papa was alive, on the mend, and it was the best Christmas present in the world. As mad as she'd been, as betrayed as she felt, those were now minor compared to losing her rock, Dutch Grantham.

Mitch walked into the room, and she immediately realized he too was a rock in her life. She felt grounded and not alone when she was with him. What would she have done without his strength and compassion these last few days?

Belle also knew she was facing the moment when she'd leave him.

And with a hole in his heart you haven't been able to fill.

But you want to, don't you?

God, yes. I want him to believe that love can again be his. I want to believe that I can fill that empty spot.

Then why do this?

Because I have to. Then I hope I can start over with Mitch. Try again.

Pain hit her hard, cramping her stomach, and she realized that she too had an empty spot that hadn't been filled since Mama's accident. And giving up the nonprofit would be nearly impossible because working on it brought her less pain.

Mitch's love would fill it.

One dream had already been squashed; she'd not allow herself to dream of Mitch loving her.

"Ready?" Mitch asked in a whisper.

"Yep. I hate to wake Junior and tell him—"

"I'm awake, Sis. Go, take a shower, and when you get back, Armie and I will hit the hotel and do the same."

"He'll be fine." She heard the doubt in her voice.

"Yes, he will. Go." Junior got up to wrap her in a hug.

Mitch steered her out of the ICU, much the same way he'd done at the United Club at the airport, a hand at the small of her back, guiding her, protecting her. He'd worn a cat-licked-the-cream expression since he'd come into Papa's ICU room, and she wondered what was up.

They walked out the hospital doors, and Belle stopped for a second to take a deep breath of the incredibly cold air, feeling it fill her, pushing out the hospital scents and fear. Then as she took another few steps with Mitch's hand still at her back, the snow began to fall.

"Snow on Christmas Eve. Looks like you will have that white Christmas." Belle paused and let the cold flakes fall onto her heated cheeks. "Do you think we could make a quick stop at maybe Target or a department store?"

"Of course. It's early enough they'll still be open."

She buckled into the SUV, and they stopped by Target. She got her small purchase, and they headed to her cabin.

He pulled up and put the car in park and was about to push off the ignition.

"You don't need to walk me to the door, I'll be fine."

The question in his eyes over her curt tone cut her to the quick. But she needed to focus on putting a barrier around her heart so her Papa wouldn't see through her and know that she was lying through her teeth.

She only needed to get through tonight.

"Okay then, pick you up in about an hour?"

She nodded and turned to open the SUV's door.

"Belle?"

She turned back to him. He leaned toward her, cupped her head to bring it closer, and covered her lips with his. A soft kiss. Yet possessive, as if telling her he was there for her.

And you'd like to believe he'd be there always.

Suddenly a ferocious need to have this kiss last forever took hold of her, and she turned the kiss into need.

He didn't back away from the change and took her lips as hungrily as she took his.

Then she broke away, layering on the armor, knowing that what she was going to do wouldn't sit well with Mitch.

FROM THE MOMENT THEY'D LEFT TARGET, BELLE BEHAVED differently. Her expression was blank, she said little and held the small gift she'd bought in a death grip. Their kiss in his car was laced with desperation.

Mitch felt her despair and knew she was going to give in to her board.

And he'd not allow that to happen.

Just what do you think you can do to stop it?

WHEN THEY ENTERED THE HOSPITAL ROOM, WORTH AND Junior were sitting with Dutch.

The older man perked up as soon as he saw Belle.

While Belle's face grew harder, more pale.

"Some Christmas Eve, huh, Princess?" Dutch said to Belle as he craned his neck as if trying to see what she held behind her back.

Belle put a tiny Christmas tree, its clear LED branches lit up with red, gold, and green, on his hospital bed table. "Since we didn't get to tramp the cabin's land in Pagosa Springs and find just the right tree, I got this. Yes, it's Christmas Eve, and I'm going to give you all the present you want."

She stood straight and moved away from Mitch, taking the center of the ICU's room. She shed the skin of the woman he'd come to love and became the princess Dutch called her.

Her face grew hard, her eyes glittered with sharp emerald facets. Worth even noticed it as he frowned and took a step toward her as if to stop her next move.

Mitch moved in front of Worth, blocking him. This was the woman he loved, and nobody was going to intercede with her but him.

Even if she hadn't given him that right by loving him. He loved her and hated this moment more than nearly anything since Lauren's death.

No more standing by wanting to fight for the people he loved but unable to help. "No—"

She turned toward him, held up her trembling hand, palm facing him.

Meaning stop.

She could have slapped him and it would hurt less.

"You've all made it quite clear that you think I'm

incapable of running Goal 100%. Since I don't have my board's support, I have nothing."

Mitch moved, only realizing it when she again held up her palm to him.

"As of January 1, I'll return any monies and close down the fund-raising portal. I will not stop the programs in progress, which I will pay for out of my own pocket. I will resign after the last class has been completed. You'll get that in writing. You gave me a choice and I'm taking this one. Not exactly as you'd decided, but it's close enough."

She turned to him and through the icy veneer Mitch saw tremendous pain and a longing that cut him to the quick. *This is not what she wants, she's made it clear. She's giving in because of Dutch's heart attack. She still believes she's at fault.*

"I will pay you for the time you've invested in this, Mitch. You are a brilliant web designer who understood my passion."

"Princess! That's—"

She held up a hand to her father. "Papa, you've already told me. I've gone over the pros and cons and I'm fine with this. My decision should relieve you of any further stress. I will find another way to help women and literacy. You know me. This is for the best. You are right, I *am* tired, discouraged—"

"That's bullshit. Sorry, Dutch and company." Mitch apologized insincerely. "Belle, you told me and I've seen you in action. You're the most alive when working on the nonprofit."

"Mitch, this isn't your concern."

15

BELLE LEFT PAPA'S ROOM, KEEPING HER TEARS AT BAY BY wrapping herself in the cloak of privilege that fit on her shoulders so uncomfortably now. She had never worn it well, but at the moment, it was the only way she could push onward.

Nor could she believe any longer in the Granthams' code of never quit; she still couldn't believe she'd been asked to do so.

But this was for the best.

It was.

"Belle."

She ignored Mitch's call.

"Belle, dammit, stop."

Glancing back she saw the only person following her out of the ICU was Mitch.

For a split moment, a glow surrounded her that he'd still be the one to follow her. That he cared enough after she'd rudely shut him off.

That she minimized the role he played in her life.

"What do you want from me?" she asked, putting as much painful distance as possible in her voice.

"Why the hell did you give in?"

Crossing her arms across her chest, she glared at him. "You know damn well why."

"You think you caused your father's heart attack."

"Well, I certainly contributed to it."

"I repeat myself, bullshit. But before we continue this conversation—"

She tried to go around him; he blocked her, stepping to the same side, and then the other as she did.

"Mitch, there is nothing more to discuss. I've made myself quite clear."

"Listen, little Miss Hoity-Toity Belle, just give me a chance and listen. Then you can go on your merry way if you don't like what I have to say."

His tone was brusque and fed up with her, yet the words warmed her soul.

She glanced at her papa's room. No one else came out. No nurses scurried in, so her pronouncement hadn't caused her papa and her board anything but relief.

"Okay, I'll listen."

MITCH STOLE GLANCES AT HER AS HE DROVE UP TO THE Davidson Mesa overlook of Boulder, the same one Belle had mentioned her family had stopped at for their first view of the city.

Mostly he got her profile, but saw her hand swipe at her face a couple of times and hated that she was so wounded by the very people she trusted.

Reaching the turnout, he pulled up to the edge of the overlook, left the SUV running for the heat, and turned in the seat to face her.

"Belle, look at the star." Through the snow, it glowed on the mountain. It was a beacon. "You asked me what I thought it meant, do you remember?"

She turned back to look at him. At her nod, he went on. "I'll tell you in a minute. Do you realize it's Christmas morn? See the sunrise just beginning to lighten the sky above the peaks?"

"And the star still glows in the shadows. It's beautiful. Thank you for bringing me here. It has great memories and this will add to them."

That sounded a bit final, yet he plowed through his uncertainty.

"I believe in you and your dream. I want you to as well."

"Mitch, you heard them—"

He put a finger to her lips. She'd shed her icy demeanor and now simply looked lost. "Now hear me. I talked to Annie, you know the—"

"New wife of Cole and author of the children's books."

Mitch nodded. "I asked her if she thought literacy for women was a cause she could support. Her answer was an instantaneous yes. She called, texted, and emailed every author she knew and in turn asked them to do the same. They want to have a once-a-year benefit where every book sold on whatever date you choose will have all the proceeds go to Goal 100%. She said right now it's about 110 authors. Big names, along with up and coming authors. They were all excited to participate—"

"Wait. You asked Annie? I thought you didn't really like her."

"I realized something in the past few days."

"What?"

A smile curved his lips. "I'll tell you in a minute or two. Jen wants to help you host a barbecue at Trickle Creek that will have some top music stars and an auction to benefit your fund. And she has the connections to get some well-heeled people with some great auction items."

He took her hand in his and brought it to his lips. "You can't give up on this dream. Do you remember asking me what I thought the star meant? Now I know. It's about believing. Believe in me. I love you. With every fiber of my being."

Belle's eyes shone with unshed tears as she shook her head.

A black doubt crept into Mitch's soul.

"How can I go back on my word now? I've told them I'm quitting. You heard me back in that room."

God help him, she didn't say she loved him in return.

He sucked up his heartache and focused on what he'd said earlier. Maybe it was too soon for her to love him. Maybe she never would. He'd still help her as much as he could. Belle Grantham filled the hole in his heart left by Lauren's death. The hole left by parents who didn't care.

The hole he'd had for a long, long time.

"Yes, I heard a woman who was afraid that she'd contributed to her father's heart attack. I heard that same woman give in because she cared enough about her father to give up her own dream. I don't know Dutch very well, but I do know that in reality, your giving up was not what he really wanted."

"I didn't believe it either, but nevertheless that's what he said."

"From the position of love. He's worried about you. And frankly I think Worth gave him an idea that they thought would be palatable to you. And honestly, parts of the idea are okay. Find a way to make it work. You *are* Goal 100%. They all know that. Find talent you can work with. Then you can focus on the part you love the most."

"Setting up the centers, helping with the training."

"Yes."

He saw the uncertainty in her eyes flee, to be replaced by a new determination.

"Do you mind if we step out of this car for a minute?" she said, offering a small smile that twisted his heart anew.

"Sure, but—"

This time she put a gentle finger to his lips.

They got out and looked at Boulder in the valley below and the star high on the mountain.

"You asked me about Annie," Mitch said. At Belle's nod, he continued. "It was simple—I was in pain, and I was afraid I'd lose my last connection to my sister. I won't. She's always with me, in my heart. Annie is a warm, generous, funny woman who will bring love and joy to my best friend, Cole, and my two nephews. How can I not love her for that alone?"

"You sound as if you're finally at peace," Belle said gently.

Not fully, not until Belle loved him. He'd fight hard for her. It was a battle he'd do his best to win. But yes, peace filled him. He'd always miss Lauren, but she'd always be with him.

"Mitch, you've given me so much the past few days. And tonight you offer me your heart."

This time all he could do was nod. The lump in his throat made it impossible to say anything.

"You filled the huge tear in my heart left by Mama's death. I only hope that I can offer you the same kind of healing."

"You already have. I think the star means hope and believing. You've given me both."

She turned him to face her. The tenseness had left her mouth, the betrayal from her eyes.

"You have my heart always. I love you, Mitchell Thomas, for now and forever. Believe in me this Christmas morn, for I believe in you."

He swept her into his arms, and covered her eyes, cheeks, and finally her lips with kisses.

"That's a pretty powerful star," he said.

"Yep. Annie had it right."

"Believe in me and my love?" Mitch asked, pulling her against him as the sun began to cast its brilliant pink light on the mountain peaks.

"Forever."

DEAR READER

I started this journey with a single book, *Be Mine This Christmas Night*, because Christmas holds a special place in my heart. Then the other characters in the book begged me to tell their stories, and this series, Star Light ~ Star Bright, was born.

Christmas has remained a special season for me, from the wonder of believing in Santa Claus as a child to the wonder of believing in the kindness and grace of the season as an adult. And since living in Boulder, Colorado, the wonder of the star on Flagstaff mountain.

Love and forgiveness seem more significant at this time of year as well.

If you enjoyed this story, please leave a review on the store's review site where you purchased it. And if you can at BookBub and Goodreads as well. We writers live or die by reviews. I know it sounds dramatic but it is so true. This is the way readers find us and buy the book.

Also, on my website www.lesliesartor.com, you can find entire *Star Light ~ Star Bright* series on the "Book Shelf" page.

And I have a newsletter that enjoy writing and sending monthly. Keeping you up to date on my writing, my crazy busy life and often my photography. And don't forget, I love hearing from you via email!

ALSO BY L. A. SARTOR

STAR LIGHT ~ STAR BRIGHT

A Romantic Christmas Series Set In Snowy Boulder, Colorado

Be Mine This Christmas Night

Forever Yours This New Year's Night

Believe In Me This Christmas Morn

Dream Of Me This Christmas Eve

THE CARSWELL ADVENTURE SERIES

Heart Pounding Adventure & Romance Set In Exotic Locales

Stone Of Heaven

Viking Gold

THE KAHUNA GROUP

Romantic Suspense With Powerful, Professional Investigators-
Offices in Hawaii ~ Denver ~ Los Angeles

Dare To Believe

Brushed By Betrayal

THE PLANTATION SERIES

Pure Romance Set in Costa Rica On A Rare Cacao Plantation

Prince Of Granola

THE JENNA HART JEWELRY MYSTERIES

A Cozy Mystery Series Set in the Colorado Ski Town Of
Angelcroft

Tick Tock Dead (coming soon)

Capture the code with a mobile device's QR reader to see all of L.A. Sartor's Books

ACKNOWLEDGMENTS

Writers work in their world, with their characters. When the book is complete it's time to send it on its way so a team of trusted people can make it the best it can be.

Thank you to ...
My treasured beta readers, **Audra Harders** and **Christine Dunning.**

My priceless editor, **Ellis Vidler.**

My mother, **Mary Sartor**, who painstakingly goes through the manuscript one last time.

And without fail, my husband, **Gary**, who always has believed in me.

ABOUT L.A. SARTOR

I started writing as a child, really. A few things happened on the way to becoming a published author ... specifically, a junior high school teacher who told me I couldn't write because I didn't want to study grammar.

That English teacher stopped my writing for years. But the muse couldn't be denied, and eventually I wrote, a lot, some of it award winning.

My husband told me repeatedly that independent publishing was becoming a valid way to publish a novel. I didn't believe him. I thought indie meant vanity press.

I couldn't have been more wrong.

I started pursuing this direction seriously, hit the keyboard, learned a litany of new things and published my first novel. My second book became a bestseller, and I'm absolutely on the right course in my life.

I live in Colorado with my husband Gary whom I met on a blind date—I can't imagine life without my best friend. We play in the mountains and travel as much as possible.

Find me at www.lesliesartor.com

DREAM OF ME THIS CHRISTMAS EVE

STAR LIGHT ~ STAR BRIGHT SERIES
BOOK FOUR

CONTROLLED CHAOS RULED THE PAST FEW HOURS. HECK, THE past few days.

Caroline Young's most important production was about to begin. Love was definitely in the air. She inhaled the fresh scents of gardenias and eucalyptus and tried to relax by remembering how this all began.

When she'd learned that children's author Annie Hamilton had fallen for Cole Evans, a widower with two young boys, Caro believed their story was the epitome of a happily ever after. Then an extra layer of joy was added as she watched Cole's brother-in-law Mitchell go from being the most negative man on the planet to a smiling best man. But Brice, the brother Caro adored, had stunned them all by thawing the Ice Queen, Jennifer Malone, who just happened to be Annie's best friend.

Caro had organized and monitored everything for the double wedding. From setting up the ginormous white tent two days ago to decorating its cavernous interior. Then making sure luxury Porta-Potties and the standby generator, which were delivered yesterday and would be working under less than ideal weather conditions, wouldn't fail, and if they did, how to troubleshoot.

Yes, this wedding used both her engineering degree and her float-building skills.

She was in her elements.

This morning she was up at five checking her lists and plans, ready for the caterers, the two coat-check attendants, and the valets. Before she dressed in her pale gray-blue silk gown, she turned on each of the table's three candles so the flickering faux flames would give extra ambiance, and if needed, just enough light for the few seconds it'd take the generator to take over if indeed the power went out.

Stop. The moment is near. Just stop.

Caro knew everything that could be under her control was taken care of. And she'd created contingencies for problems. The snow that continued to fall, while gorgeous, added a major headache to the day.

Then again, it was mid-December in Boulder, Colorado, and it snowed here.

Fidgeting with her bridesmaid bouquet, then checking the clock she'd placed discreetly at the entrance to the tent, she saw it was finally 12 p.m. sharp. A second later she heard her cue as RJ, their good friend and pianist for the ceremony, switched from playing his soft piano music and started playing Clarke's Trumpet Voluntary. It was time.

Caro turned and looked behind her. First stood Cole's

boys, Josh and Peter, followed by the brides. "Are you ready?" she whispered to Jennifer and Annie.

"Couldn't have done it without you, wild child," Jen teased.

"Seriously?" Caro rolled her eyes. "I thought that name was dead and buried."

Feeling a tug on her dress, Caro looked down.

"What's a wild child?" Josh asked.

Caro widened her eyes and stared hard at Jen, who winked in reply, before answering the boy. "I'll tell you later."

"Okay."

She took a deep breath, knowing this was going to be an incredible day.

Grinning, she directed the boys, looking serious and adorable in their gray suits, to begin. Each had the duty of being a ring bearer for one couple. She followed behind them, starting her step-pause-step cadence down the white, fabric-covered aisle.

Caro's smile widened as she saw her brother standing on the grooms' side, craning his neck to look behind her. He obviously couldn't wait to see his bride, Jennifer Malone.

Beside him stood Cole, impatiently waiting for his bride, Annie Hamilton.

Reaching the altar Caro had decorated with fairy lights, pine boughs, white gardenias and Phalaenopsis orchids, silvery eucalyptus leaves and swaths of silver netting, the boys stood next to the grooms and their uncle

Mitchell, acting as dual best man. She moved to the brides' side.

RJ paused for a beat, then played fortissimo, and the two hundred guests rose to honor the two brides, best friends since childhood, as they started down the aisle, side by side.

Caro knew that neither of the women had plans to fall in love and get married. Cupid had other ideas. She'd heard both the couples' stories several times, and it never ceased to amaze her that people could fall in love in such a short time. She'd stopped believing in fairy tales about the age of ten. Yet, here was her brother with Jen, and Cole with Annie.

Just before the brides arrived at the altar, Caro glanced at her parents in the front row. Her mom fumbled with the white hanky Dad handed her, then wiped away tears of joy. They too had fallen in love quickly in the small Kansas town where Caro and Brice had grown up.

Caro returned her attention to the couples in front of her and took the two bouquets, stepping back as the grooms joined their brides.

RJ rose from the piano and stood before them. He'd been ordained especially for this day.

This wedding, a week shy of Christmas, had been in the planning stages for about six months. Caro would have dropped any clients for Forever Young, her business, that wouldn't allow her the luxury of a week off from their projects to attend this celebration. Last year she'd had her first float in the prestigious Rose Bowl parade in Pasadena and even won an award for it. She had another one for the parade a year away, but from a couple of days ago to December twenty-seventh, she had a clean slate and promised to spend Christmas in Boulder.

Her dance card was full with a crazy, demanding job, but one she loved.

Her attention focused back on the wedding as Brice took a ring from Josh, Cole's youngest son.

"You are my life, my love. Forever is not long enough to show you the depth of my admiration and love for you," her brother vowed to his beloved.

He slipped the ring on Jennifer's finger and swept her into a dip-style kiss.

The guests applauded and hooted, then Jennifer and Brice, hand in hand, stepped aside, making room for Annie, Cole, and the boys to stand in front of RJ.

Cole clasped Annie's hands. "Annie, Josh and Peter adore you. I love you and believe I'm the luckiest man in the world to have you by our sides, in our lives, believing in our dreams as we move through life together," Cole vowed.

Peter handed Cole a ring, and he slipped it on Annie's finger, then kissed her soundly. She bent to embrace the boys and give them each a kiss.

Tears unexpectedly flooded Caro's eyes at the bounty of love that emanated from this tiny spot in the universe.

The lights in the chandeliers flickered and, much to her relief, stayed lit. RJ played a rousing tune as the couples, followed by the boys, then Caro, with her hand tucked in Mitchell's arm, walked up the aisle.

Just before she ducked into the house, Caro heard RJ announce to the guests that while the couple signed documents and the chairs were being moved to the tables, the wine bar and coffee bar were open if people would like to enjoy.

She followed the wedding party into Jennifer's dining room. As she was adding her witness signature to each of the documents, the lights flickered once again, then stayed off.

MAXIMILLIAN HENDERSON III ADMIRED HOW THE cavernous tent filled with two hundred-plus guests felt intimate, yet exotic.

His sense of aesthetics approved of the eucalyptus garlands snaking down the center of the oak tables. White blooms of some sort and ribbons of silver netting intertwined with the best faux candles he'd ever seen casting their flickering light. China, silverware, and soft white linen napkins sat on oak tables.

The effect was both elegant and eclectic.

As was the creator of all this, bridesmaid Caroline Young in her filmy gown and tumbled fiery hair.

Max was Jen's next-door neighbor, and when Brice had come into the picture, they'd become friends. Often, over dinner, drinks, or a movie trivia night, Brice talked about his sister and had proudly shown Max many pictures of her.

He'd been fascinated by the way she so easily, and with insouciance, wore combinations of patterns, textures, and colors. None of the woman he knew could carry off the bohemian look that flattered this fiery sprite.

In fact, he recognized a bit of envy in his admiration of her. He wore suits to work and well-thought-out casual clothes, and pretty much everything he wore matched. Her "look" felt much more carefree than his attorney persona would allow. And damn if he didn't admire her freedom to dress as she chose. Maybe if he could spend a bit of time with her, it'd rub off on him.

Max, old man, you've carefully cultivated this attorney persona. Don't forget that.

Right. Yet her magic lingered as he looked down at his dark suit, then thought of her in her flowing maid-of-honor gown.

Damn, now you're being fanciful.

Suddenly, the chandeliers in the tent flickered, then went dark, the only light now twinkling from the candles on the tables and wan winter light coming from the tent's clear plastic windows. Murmurs around him were more curious than anxious.

Moments later, through the windows Max saw Caro moving like a wisp of gray smoke along the outside of the tent. She'd donned a gray sweater over her gown and covered her hair with a muffler of some sort.

Then she disappeared from sight as the falling snow enveloped her. What the heck was she doing?

Instantly he was on his feet and headed through the nearly invisible door at the back of the tent. Spur of the moment wasn't his style. Nothing about Caro was his style, yet he felt suddenly and completely protective of her. It was bitterly cold, still snowing, and she was out there alone.

And on top of his worry, there was something about her that spiraled a tendril of desire through him. Just a hint, nothing he could pin down, but enough to add urgency to his quest.

Snow immediately filled his shoes and came midway up his calves as he forged a path through the virgin snow, heading in the direction he last saw Caro take. Finally, he was on the plowed driveway and could now make time as he passed the trailer of fancy Porta-Potties. A few feet beyond that and he was back in deeper snow.

Following the trail of footsteps, he finally found Caro bending over a mammoth generator, which thankfully was running. Yet she remained beside it.

"Need some help?"

She looked up, then dusted her hands off and tucked them beneath her sweater.

"Nope, think I found the issue. The Porta-Potti wagon must have rolled over the electrical cord enough to pull it from its emergency socket. The power should be on by now."

She made a move to retrace her steps to check on the lights in the tent when he saw her shiver. He at least had on a wool suit coat. And while her sweater looked warm, the gray dress beneath it didn't. "I'll go look, you head to Jennifer's lab and get warm before we head back."

"I've got on boots—you don't. But I would like to double-check a couple things on my planning board, so thank you."

He looked down, and damn if she didn't have on heavy boots under her bridesmaid gown. "I'll meet you at the lab in a minute."

"I don't need you to—"

Max didn't wait to hear her answer as he retraced his steps far enough to see the lights in the tent. He could go on and enjoy the party, as he was sure Caro had been going to say, yet he paused.

What on earth caused that? Was it the emotion of the double wedding, the closeness of Christmas? Whatever the reason, desire to know Caro a whole lot better struck him hard.

He waited in the falling snow and bitter cold to see if his desire to be near her still hammered at him, and realized it hammered harder.

Okay then. Back to Jen's pool house, which she'd turned into a mini version of her forensics office she called the lab.

He entered quietly and softly shut the door behind him. Caroline hadn't heard him, thus offering him time to study her. She'd pulled off the muffler and wore her hair in a messy sort of style, while an embroidered headband studded with gemstones of some sort held the fiery mass off her face. The bluish gray of her gown fit her style perfectly.

While she appeared delicate, he knew otherwise from the times Brice had talked about her welding part of a float if she was short a person or climbing up on the skeleton to add the wire mesh that would hold the flowers. Or driving hell-bent through a corn field in Kansas as a teenager.

Brice called her a wild child.

Max's glance flicked over to the wall to see what she appeared to be engrossed in. Flow charts, lists, and schematics covered the entire wall over the desk. "This looks like a battle plan."

Caro turned, and her smile practically knocked him backward. It was completely genuine all the way to the sparkle in her gray eyes. She was obviously in her element. He understood, for he felt that way when he won a case or created a complex trust or complicated real estate lease.

Her energy drew him closer, and he had to stop from touching her, though his fingers itched to trace the column of her throat to her jaw and then down again, to her—

"Well, since I couldn't talk either couple out of a winter wedding, I had to plan for every contingency." She waved her hands toward the wall of plans and charts.

Max stepped even closer to take a better look.

He studied the plans tacked up and suddenly realized this woman could be exactly what he needed.

Now all he had to do was think of a way to convince her.

"Ready to go back?" he asked, formulating and discarding ideas even as he spoke.

"Yep, but your shoes didn't get dry."

"It's okay, I'll survive."

Caro laughed. A throaty, full-bodied sound he felt all the way to his cold toes.

"Some wine, champagne, and a great meal combined with all this love will warm you up." Caro rose and wrapped her muffler back around her neck and over her head.

"Are you a romantic?"

"Only for other people."

What an odd thing for her to say.